Praise for *Water Ghosts* by S

"In her notably assured debut, *Wate[
explores the uneasy confluence of assimilation and ancestry in
the lives of these immigrants. . . . Ryan is artful in examin-
ing matters of race, class, gender, sexual preference, and culture,
resisting the doctrinaire and prescriptive in her writing, and avoid-
ing any politicization of the issues. Her prose undulates grace-
fully, exuding an impressionistic, almost hallucinogenic mood,
as if the story is taking place in a dream. . . . Ryan's subtle use of
water and ghosts as intertwined motifs of the ancestral is drawn
from Chinese myths and deftly crafted, while her vignettes from
prior years are seamlessly placed. The novel pulses, with the past
continually surging against the present until the present yields.
In *Water Ghosts*, Ryan has distinguished herself as a writer to
watch."   —*The Boston Globe*

"Ryan explores love, desire, loss, and betrayal as she combines
history and myth in lyrical prose that is both delicate and sensu-
ous. An accomplished and affecting first novel."   —*Booklist*

"A dreamlike haze shimmers over Ryan's debut, the tale of a real-
life immigrants' enclave in early twentieth-century California. . . .
Ryan's fluid flashbacks allow the past to sweep over the collective
population of Locke, and her elegant female protagonists manage to exercise their own agency even when they're hemmed in by
life in Locke."   —*Publishers Weekly*

"Using a handful of characters, debut novelist Ryan offers impres-
sions of a Chinese American community in 1920s California. . . .
Fascinating."   —*Kirkus Reviews*

"Artfully woven, exquisitely modulated, walking a master's line
between ancient Chinese myth and the grit of immigrant life
in the Sacramento Delta, *Water Ghosts* tells the unforgettable
story of a town brought to its knees by loneliness and longing.

Complicated, compassionate, haunting, Shawna Ryan's novel feels more like tapestry than words on paper, her prose less like sentences, and more like song."

—Pam Houston, author of *Cowboys Are My Weakness*

"Shawna Ryan's *Water Ghosts* is a multilayered marvel of a book. The prose is a delight, the characters fascinating, the story richly imagined and heart-rending. This first novel of grace and substance presages a notable literary career for Shawna Ryan."

—John Lescroart, author of *The Hunt Club*

"*Water Ghosts* is an auspicious debut that not only entertains, but opens our eyes to a rich, poignant piece of Chinese American history."   —Gail Tsukiyama, author of *Dreaming Water*

"A beautiful debut, *Water Ghosts* opens up a page in history that sometimes is forgotten by both cultures that once coexisted in Locke, a Sacramento Chinese farming town. By mapping out the familiar and the strange territories of human passion and retelling the old myths, Shawna Yang Ryan tells a story that, in the end, is about how America was truly made."

—Yiyun Li, author of *A Thousand Years of Good Prayers*

"This is potent, deeply felt, magical writing. . . . Don't miss this book."   —Gary Snyder, Pulitzer Prize–winning poet and author of *Mountains and Rivers Without End*

"Shawna Yang Ryan writes with even frightening intimacy about: preachers, bootleggers, prostitutes, ghosts, and an utterly convincing soothsaying madame. Every word she writes about their storied, haunted, fogbanked Sacramento River town rings absolutely true. Savor *Water Ghosts*, this brilliant incarnation of the California novel, and you'll be amply, richly rewarded. Just to read it will ruin you for Steinbeck."

—John Beckman, author of *The Winter Zoo*

PENGUIN BOOKS

WATER GHOSTS

Shawna Yang Ryan was born and raised in Northern California. *Water Ghosts*, originally published as *Locke 1928*, was a finalist for the 2008 Northern California Book Award. She currently lives in Berkeley.

Water Ghosts

Shawna Yang Ryan

PENGUIN BOOKS

PENGUIN BOOKS
Published by the Penguin Group
Penguin Group (USA) Inc., 375 Hudson Street, New York, New York 10014, U.S.A.
Penguin Group (Canada), 90 Eglinton Avenue East, Suite 700, Toronto,
Ontario, Canada M4P 2Y3 (a division of Pearson Penguin Canada Inc.)
Penguin Books Ltd, 80 Strand, London WC2R 0RL, England
Penguin Ireland, 25 St Stephen's Green, Dublin 2, Ireland (a division of Penguin Books Ltd)
Penguin Group (Australia), 250 Camberwell Road, Camberwell,
Victoria 3124, Australia (a division of Pearson Australia Group Pty Ltd)
Penguin Books India Pvt Ltd, 11 Community Centre, Panchsheel Park, New Delhi – 110 017, India
Penguin Group (NZ), 67 Apollo Drive, Rosedale, North Shore 0632,
New Zealand (a division of Pearson New Zealand Ltd)
Penguin Books (South Africa) (Pty) Ltd, 24 Sturdee Avenue,
Rosebank, Johannesburg 2196, South Africa

Penguin Books Ltd, Registered Offices:
80 Strand, London WC2R 0RL, England

First published in the United States of America by The Penguin Press,
a member of Penguin Group (USA) Inc. 2009
Published in Penguin Books 2010

1   3   5   7   9   10   8   6   4   2

Originally published under the title *Locke 1928* by El Leon Literary Arts

Excerpts from *The Nobel Acceptance Speech* by Toni Morrison, Alfred A. Knopf, 1994.

PUBLISHER'S NOTE
This is a work of fiction. Names, characters, places, and incidents are either the product
of the author's imagination or are used fictitiously, and any resemblance to actual persons,
living or dead, business establishments, events, or locales is entirely coincidental.

THE LIBRARY OF CONGRESS HAS CATALOGED THE HARDCOVER EDITION AS FOLLOWS:
Ryan, Shawna Yang, date.
Water ghosts : a novel / Shawna Yang Ryan.
p.   cm.
ISBN 978-1-59420-207-0 (hc.)
ISBN 978-0-14-311727-8 (pbk.)
1. Chinese—California—Delta Region—Fiction.   2. Immigrants—California—Delta Region—
Fiction.   3. Locke (Calif.)—Fiction.   4. Delta Region (Calif.)—Fiction.   I. Title.
PS3618.Y344L63 2009
813'.6—dc22   2008029400

Printed in the United States of America
Designed by Stephanie Huntwork

For my parents, Mike and Ellen

Tell us what it is to be a woman so that we may know what it is to be a man. What moves at the margin. What it is to have no home in this place. To be set adrift from the one you knew. What it is to live at the edge of towns that cannot bear your company.

—TONI MORRISON
Nobel lecture, December 7, 1993

PRINCIPAL CHARACTERS

Richard Fong (aka Fong Man Gum), *manager of the Lucky
    Fortune Gambling Hall*
Ming Wai, *Richard's wife, one of three boat-women*
Poppy See (aka Po Pei), *brothel madam, seer*
Chloe Virginia Howell, *a prostitute in Madam See's brothel,
    Richard Fong's lover*
Howar Lee, *preacher*
Corlissa Lee, *wife of preacher Howar Lee*
Sofia Lee, *their only daughter, friend of Chloe's*
So Wai, *boat-woman*
Sai Fung, *boat-woman*

MINOR CHARACTERS

Alfred, *Chloe's former lover*
Barrett, *Chloe's former admirer*
Lee Bing, *founder of Locke*
Tuffy Leamon, *speakeasy owner*
Uncle Happy, *farm laborer*
Cholly Wong, *ill-fated rescuer of boat-women*
Manny Chow, *gambler*
Mrs. Chow, *bootlegger, wife of Manny Chow*
Lau Sing Yan, *Richard Fong's childhood friend and rival*
Sarah, *Poppy See's fellow dancer, adulteress*
The butcher, *Sarah's lover, murderer*
Ruby Moore, *New York jazz singer*
David Howell, *Chloe's brother*
Jack Yang, *restaurant owner*
Lucy Yang, *Jack Yang's wife*

The Founding (1915)

HER MIND WAS taken with the thought of pussy willows. She saw them in the market, long cut stems emerging from a bucket of water, ten cents a bunch. Each fistful tied with string. Her eyes lingered over them as she stood in line with a can of condensed milk. She weighed the can in her hand as she thought about the willows—which vase she might use, which corner or tabletop they might decorate. She lived in a small apartment—kitchen crowding into dining area crowding into sitting space crowding into a room for a bed. That was all. The way the light fell, through thick glass windows onto tea-colored walls, would turn the brown branches gold.

She thought of them as she lit the oil stove. The newspaper that covered the wall behind the stove was ready to be replaced. Yellowed already, torn, grease-splattered to a high sheen—it had done its job. Her mind brushed over the task for a moment, then forgot it when she thought of the blooms that could be added to the vase. The motions of lunch making were gone through—measuring, adding, flavoring, stirring—as she lost herself in the idea of color. Lime-colored leaves, petals from heart-red to eggshell-blue. The little wood platform the stove rested on rocked as she moved her chopsticks. The wedge of wood scrap supporting the too-short leg had slipped out again. She leaned to nudge it back into place.

The sizzle of cooking oil obscured the sound of sparks lifting and catching. She stood up and slid her chopsticks along the thick black pan and the sweep of her hand was met by the sudden sweep of flames up the wall, up the old newspaper. She shrieked and grabbed for a bowl of water. Her frantic turn knocked over the stove. She tossed water on the fire; it sputtered and grew. She tried again and again. The fire spread across the wall, licked at the ceiling.

IN THE STREET, she huddled close to her neighbors and cried as they watched the fire spread from building to building. Although the river was only a few hundred yards away, the task of bringing water to fire was beaten by the strong north wind. The fireboats struggled. The people relied on yelling— shouting from Japantown into Chinatown for everyone to flee. Both would char and crumple.

The fire grew so fast that no one except the woman who daydreamed of flowers was sure of its origin. The Chinese would say it began with the Japanese; the Japanese would claim the opposite. And both would live for days with the stench of toppled wood and of the burnt flesh of men too opium-addled to escape.

I

STRANGE HAPPENINGS, CHLOE knows, can take place in a town built on tragedy. After the Chinatown fire in Walnut Grove, the Chung Shan Chinese moved over to the Locke family property to start over. The first building had been a store. A boardinghouse and gambling hall followed until a community had arisen and clustered around the three buildings. The town was called Lockeport, then, eventually, as tongues grew lazy and letters were lost: Locke.

Thirteen years after the original fire, Chloe feels made and unmade by the air in the two-road town. She has been turned into something new from sleeping alongside the other girls in the attic of Madam See's brothel to the sound of bats fluttering in the eaves-spaces. She is of an untouchable caste, even as she lies now in the red room with Richard Fong's head resting on her chest. Tule fog presses against the windows and obscures the faint dawn light. It is summer, but the room is cold and gray, the lamp wick extinguished for hours already. The dark borders of the room, lingering like shadow people, push in around the bed. In the dimness, Chloe sees only Richard, jawbone and lips to make you cry and eyes dark as Valentino's; the mellowed pink tint of the sheets; and the cold hurricane lamp on the nightstand. Richard asks her to say his name.

She responds, Richard.

No. Fong Man Gum.

Chloe's voice flattens out the curves, Fong Man Gum.

Once more.

Fong Man Gum.

He grows hard inside her.

Fong Man Gum.

He breathes in her ear; his breath staggers and falters.

Fong Man Gum.

His sighs collapse in jags into the curve of her neck.

Chloe lifts her hands and drags her fingers through his hair, pulls lightly; she wants him to hush, even as she utters his name a final time.

Fong Man Gum.

IT IS JUNE 22, 1928, and the morning of the Dragon Boat Festival. Back pressed to the wall, Poppy See can feel the vibrations of Richard's footsteps move down the hall. She smokes as she listens. She would like to sleep, but a premonition has awoken her: bodies with seaweed-strewn faces under water, glistening and pale, with bloated fingers and Delta crawdads scuttling though the water-heavy locks of their hair. She hoped it had been a dream, or even a memory—in her youth, shamed women had been pulled from the river with some regularity—but when she rose and turned on the light, she discovered that the bowl of dry rice at her small altar had been disturbed and the incense sticks lay broken.

Flooded with light, the room looked otherwise normal, but she couldn't stop the bird in her chest, so she went to the wall to wait for him. For four years she had opened her eyes to Richard's face and had inhaled his rank night breath in order to know that the horrors of sleep could dissipate with him sleeping beside her. Before she heard his footsteps, she heard the groan and ease of springs as he left Chloe's bed.

Through her thin nightdress and the ridges of the wall, she feels his feet crack past her room. Fingers smash cigarette into gold dish. She leaps to open the door. His figure—jacket uncreased and tight across his back, the drape of his pants over the curve of his heel—retreats down the hall. Disappointment draws her heart into a beating-wing frenzy, but the next sight stills her. Behind Richard follows a woman in an old-style dress—snapped-closed collar, sleeves falling wide like bells, and, beneath the embroidered hem of her dress, tiny bound feet. Against the harsh outlines of Richard's suit, the woman is so delicate she follows like an echo to a sound. Richard descends the stairs, but the woman pauses and turns to look at Poppy. Poppy freezes. Hand to the doorknob, legs in indecision as she weighs this against her visions. Through the woman's soft girlish face, Poppy continues to watch Richard's fleeing figure.

THE CHILDREN WILL collect at the southern end of Main Street, near the slough and railroad tracks. The domestic quiet of Second Street slinks into the chaos of Main. Under the sycamores and willows, cars line the one-lane road. The stores will have lifted their blinds and opened their doors to the raised wooden sidewalks that fall in and out of light beneath the balconies.

It is nine and the fog is gone. Corlissa climbs the stairs to rouse her daughter Sofia for the parade. She knocks on the door. When there is no response, she hesitates to enter. She feels the headiness that often had come to her when she looked down from the window of their apartment in the city. The spin when each stone of the alley looked impossibly close, then dizzily far. All the dares that arise in a playing mind: to leap in front of a streetcar, to walk into the ocean with a pocket full of stones, to step out the window—initially came to her when she held her baby daughter. After Sofia learned to walk, the thoughts came on their own, and Corlissa learned to hold her breath when crossing the street, to count out the seconds until the cars passed.

She glances down the hall toward her own bedroom door, ajar, room empty. Perhaps if Sofia had been a son the thoughts wouldn't have come. Fifteen years later, they arrive even more often, now that Sofia's body presses against her clothes and threatens to burst out with hips and breasts and blood and milk. The lack of traffic and tall buildings in Locke doesn't stop Corlissa's urges, and the confusion that swirls around her—the only whitewoman in town not a prostitute—brings the flush of danger rising higher. Red-haired and freckled, she feels conspicuous, like a rag doll left in the street. Each corner she turns in her seven-months-new town offers another solution. She's found an oak tree with branches that will hold a body; the gas released from an unlit oven is intoxicating; and, of course, the river is only a few hundred feet away.

She knocks again. No answer from Sofia's room. She nudges the door open.

Sofia disappears for hours each day and gives vague replies when asked where she's been. Summer allows for roaming, but the waves descend on Corlissa when Sofia comes home, noncommittal in her answers, and smelling odd-musky. Corlissa has not made enough friends in town for it to be whispered to her what her daughter is up to. She is unsettled enough to feel chilled at night when she thinks of this creature, her daughter, from her own body, who sleeps down the hall, in the dark mystery of her room.

Behind Sofia's door, discarded socks lie on the floor, a magazine splays under the bed, and fragrance lingers in the air amid the haze of morning light that washes the room. The cover is pulled over the bed, but still rumpled. The blue and green flowers printed across it wink like flirting eyes. A

basket of gimcrackery sits on the nightstand—metal snap-
pers, ceramic sheep, a high-bouncing ball. Sofia is still such a
girl. All the trimmings of girlhood mark the room, but there
is no girl here.

EVEN WITHOUT ATTENDING, Chloe knows how the
festivities will go: the children will carry banners and flags and
dragon puppets made of felt and paper stuck together with
paste. The painted ten-year-old girls in majorette costumes—
cheeks rosy, lips red, faces powdered—will lead off with high
kicks and twirls and faces upturned toward thrown batons.
And the older boys in dragon masks will line the route, baring
white paper teeth.

The merchants will stand in the doorways of their busi-
nesses, pulled by the merrymaking, but still reluctant to count
out the till and close the shop. People from Walnut Grove,
Courtland, Ryde, Isleton, will arrive in straw boater hats,
vests, picnic-day dresses, to see the exotic spectacle played out
in their own homeland.

Cable-armed farm laborers culled in from the fields and
orchards, fingers crooked from pruning shears and wrists ach-
ing from asparagus pulling, will bring up the rear, carrying
boats. They will march toward the water by following the flash
of little girls' ankle socks glimpsed from under the shadow-
hollow of the upside-down boat held above their heads.

Then the plash of wood hitting water. The thunder of heels

hitting wood. The ung! of men rowing wood oars through water to a steady drumbeat.

A RATTLE OF pebbles across the window startles Chloe. Sofia waits below, dressed like a sailor girl. She glances over a shoulder draped in a big blue collar, then beckons Chloe down.

Downstairs, Chloe eases past Madam See's closed office door and onto the stoop.

Let's go, Sofia says. I can't stand those kids. Her little freckled nose edges up into a snarl. She has told Chloe about the girls, so friendly to each other, who shift at her approach, reconfiguring themselves until Sofia sees only touching shoulders and the napes of smooth necks. Not even a look. Months ago, Sofia said, she'd thought it was San Francisco all over again, where she was dragged from white school to white school until she found herself at school in Chinatown, among children who thought half white was a half too much. But in Locke, there was no taunting. It all happened in whispers and, then, in silence.

I'm not supposed to be gone, Chloe says.

C'mon, Chloe, the whole town is closing down. Let's go to the river.

Chloe sighs, What about the parade?

I don't care. Mama isn't going anyhow.

They peer around the corner at the growing crowd, then run along the railroad tracks to the slough that curves behind the town. They skid-skad their heels down the bank, through soft mud and strands of creeping wild rye. Chloe and Sofia climb onto a low branch that overhangs the dirt and water. Two girls, one blond and one brown-haired, perch on a branch with legs dangling.

You got smokes? Sofia asks.

Chloe loosens a pouch of Prince Albert tobacco and rolling papers from her garter and hands them to Sofia.

I've been thinking about what your mother said last week.

Sofia licks the paper flap and picks a fleck of tobacco off her tongue. Matches?

Chloe takes matches from her left garter.

Sofia says, I don't know how you stand being so far away from things. I'm out of my mind here.

I thought you didn't like the city.

Sometimes I do.

What's it like being saved? Chloe asks.

I don't remember; I was little.

I want to be.

Jesus Christ, Sofia says. She blows out a long streamer of smoke, affecting glamour.

I don't want to live here all my life either. What's it like?

It's like taking a bath.

Chloe takes off her shoes and hooks them on a branch, unfastens her garters, and unrolls her stockings, leaving them hanging. She hops down, calf-deep in brown-green water.

Show me what it's like. She bends and trails her fingers in the water; water rolls by, cool.

Stop, Chloe.

Chloe looks up at Sofia and swats her ankle. Sofia, Big-City Sofia, show me what it's like.

Sofia flings her cigarette into the river. She pulls off her shoes and drops in next to Chloe. She faces Chloe. The light plays through the leaves and flutters across her face.

Get down.

Chloe kneels.

Chloe Virginia Howell, do you reject Satan and all his empty promises? Then Sofia whispers, You say, I do.

I do.

Do you accept Jesus as your Lord and Savior?

I do.

Sofia moves to Chloe's side, her right hand behind Chloe's head, her left on Chloe's breastbone, and slowly pushes Chloe backward.

You're going under now, she whispers.

The water slides over Chloe's face and she holds her eyes open for as long as she can. Sofia hovers above her, figure distorted by water. Trust seeps from Chloe's pliant body to Sofia, and Sofia begins to shake, pushes harder.

She's losing her breath. Chloe grabs for Sofia and Sofia pulls her up from the ice, back into the warm day. Chloe's eyes tear from the sting of cold and silt.

That which is born of the flesh is flesh; you must be born again, Sofia whispers. You're saved.

Chloe breathes hard. She climbs onto the branch and looks at Sofia while she twists water from her dress.

Were you scared?

No. There is a long pause as Chloe keeps her eyes on Sofia.

The first revelers begin to line the bank.

We should go, Chloe says.

No, Sofia says. Stay here.

2

WHEN POPPY APPROACHES Richard on the riverbank, the anxieties of the morning return. Large black hat pulled low across her right eye, she glides up next to him. Heat rises from her heart to her neck and floods up from chin to cheeks. Scents spin off his body, so strong they are almost visible to her—the slick, wax smell of Brylcreem in his hair; the sweat coming through his suit; body scent, unrelieved by soap and cologne, that lingers behind his ears and in the lines of his throat.

She greets him with a tentative smile.

He turns his head in his slow and easy way and says hello as if she's merely a cat rubbing persistently against his legs.

I didn't see you this morning.

I was by.

You should have stopped in on your way out. She says it lightly.

I had to get back to the Lucky Fortune.

Poppy presses her lips together and nods. The sun passes through the trees. Everything grows hotter. Prickles of heat rise up Poppy's back, underneath the cool feel of her silk dress. She places a hand on Richard's arm to steady herself.

Are you all right?

She nods and closes her eyes. The feeling settles and she sorts it out in the pause: a home in China with brick floors and round doorways. Richard's gaze met by the eyes of a body afloat. She hears his name spoken from the mouth of a teenage girl.

Richard fans Poppy with his hat: Summer comes with a vengeance; let's go in the shade.

Under the shade of an oak, Richard says, I'll be going home soon. Maybe Chloe mentioned it?

Poppy says nothing.

To see my wife.

Poppy's head throbs. She watches the unsteady boats bobbing toward some semblance of a starting line, trying to ease their bows straight and even. She asks, Will you come back?

I don't think so.

Richard turns from her to watch the river. A man stands in tentative balance in one boat. He rolls up his shirtsleeves, tosses a toothpick in the water, and shouts something that makes his oarsmen laugh. The conversations around them flatten out as people turn toward the river in anticipation of the starter's gun. A girl tosses rice into the water to satiate the fish. It's a talisman against the myth: the dragon boats reenact the lifeboats sent to find the drowned hero-poet, whose body was fed upon by fish. The oarsmen toss paper money into the water now to appease any lurking spirits. The drummers bend around, stretch their torsos, and stuff the dragons' mouths full of money. On shore, fireworks explode to scare water spirits who might lie in wait.

The popping of the firecrackers intensifies the ache in Poppy's head. She presses her fingers to her forehead and tries to rub out the pain.

You might.

What? Richard looks at her again. She blushes, ashamed at the relief imparted by his gaze.

You might come back.

He turns back to the river as if disappointed by her banality. He says, I'll leave money for Chloe.

Chloe can take care of herself.

At a gunshot, the boats are off. The spectators shout with delight as the oars push through water, fight currents. Each boat represents a Delta product. There are the asparagus men, the pear pickers, the tomato laborers. The pear pickers inch in front of the asparagus men, but then, biceps strong from digging, the asparagus men pull ahead. The tomato boat drifts behind. The money offering flutters loose from the dragon's mouth and melts into the water. The shouting on shore grows to a roar. Suddenly, despite the cheers, all rowing stops and paddles skim the surface of the water. Black clouds roll over the sun and shade the hot June day. All boats are lost, unsure whether to proceed. The river—animals and people and water—falls silent. Poppy, hot and sure she's in the throes of another vision, this one so strong the whole town engages, faints.

. . .

WHEN THE SKY goes dark, Sofia says, It's going to rain? She steps out from under the tree and holds out her palm. It's going to rain?

Chloe does not answer. She watches spinning boats and revelers with heads angled in curiosity and, beyond them, a mist that creeps over the silty water. It bathes the slough in the color of dawn. As the wave of clouds tides in from the range to the west, a bank of fog creeps down the river from the north. It swallows the light and land in its path.

I said it's going to rain, Sofia repeats.

Chloe's eyes are drawn to the black, black center of the fog, at some pulsating thing trying to birth its way through.

Sofia, Chloe says, look at the river.

THE FOG DRIFTS quickly through the still air, carried on an unfelt breeze. The fog obscures the finish line and the rowers have stopped. Their oars skim the water, a smack smack as they bounce over small ripples and slap the surface again. The fog's dark center laces their blood with reluctance. They try to turn the boats away. But the drummers, their backs to the fog, keep pounding out their rowing rhythms, palms against taut-hide barrel drums. They beat with insistence and wonder, each one dumbfounded at the oarsmen's apathy.

Those on the banks, whose attentions have shifted from

the boats to the fog, bring their hands to their mouths and noses. It is a gesture of horror propelled by the stink.

The smell is a prelude. For Richard, it hearkens back to a hot August day fifteen years past: his father's body laid out in the parlor, puddles of melted ice beneath him. Mourners dressed in white, all windows open, but even the crossbreeze couldn't undercut the humidity. When the funeralgoers passed by the body with handkerchiefs held up to their noses, Richard shifted, embarrassed.

For some, the fog steam smells like salmon dead from the effort of spawning, and rotting in the November sun on the banks of a river. For others, it is salt-encrusted heels flecked with sand after a day at the beach. And to some, it is afterbirth boiled into a broth for new mothers.

Stillness descends. The dragon boats, caught in a spiraling current, spin in lazy circles. Mothers hunch down beside their children and whisper nonsensical assurances in their ears; men shift their legs in preparation to either fight or flee.

The dark center breaks through the heaving belly of fog. What spills forth, in a shimmer, is a tattered boat.

Eighty-four-year-old Cholly Wong finds himself twenty-one again, in October 1865, on the day he helped pull bodies from the water. The *Yosemite*, a steamer, had just left its dock on the riverside when the boiler exploded. The sky filled with people, wood, and metal. Those in the China hold, the section next to the boiler, bore the brunt of the explosion. The pieces of their bodies were sent first to the river's bottom before they floated slowly to the surface. They've floated again, bodies held down for years now free for burial. Cholly pushes at his sleeves with hands stained with liver spots and braces for the cold water.

Richard, crouched next to Poppy's limp body, turns toward the water. The boat carries three women. Badly dressed, but he can still discern curves and long strands of hair falling loose from upsweeps. Runaway prostitutes. Singsong girls, tramps. And a valuable load—it costs over a thousand dollars to smuggle in just one. Richard arches at the thought of conflict—if the boat lands here, someone will inevitably follow. Will it be worth it to be run after with knives and guns? Better to let them drift on to another destination. He presses the back of his hand to Poppy's forehead and murmurs, Wake up, wake up.

Behind closed lids, Poppy waits a moment longer, reluctant to be pulled into the silent chaos around her. Behind closed lids, she experiences a different sort of premonition: All she has worked for since her escape—from a man who was to be her husband but became her broker—taken from her, piece by piece, dollar by dollar. The freedom she bought, through slick thighs, and a disease that scarred her womb; the business she built—all gone, taken by a presence whose borders she can't quite feel out. Let her stay in this moment, deaf to the swirl, for just a heartbeat longer.

CHLOE CLIMBS PAST Sofia. She cranes her neck, searching through the gray. She climbs higher, steadies her bare feet against bark. Emerging finally through the leafy top, she follows the line of the water down toward the fogbank. She sees a tattered craft, and aboard—one, two, three!—goddesses stepped down from heaven. She makes up details to match paintings she has seen: regal backed in black gowns, hair twisted up and held with hand-hammered silver combs, ears that dangle glass baubles. She hears her breath above the lap and slosh of water and is suddenly aware of the heat, the gloriousness of the heat, which has, for eighteen days straight, elicited comments from everyone she passed in the street and through the discomfort made her aware of her skin. She pauses for a moment in the wonder of it, then clambers down the tree again, foot sliding just once, and hears Sofia say, We have to go there.

THE BOAT DRIFTS closer and closer, gliding past the dragon boats and their gape-jawed rowers. The women's vague faces grow more defined as the fog recedes. Mirage becomes real. As the boat bobs past the pier, the townspeople pick out the details that mark the women as solid: the tangled hair, the sunburnt and salt-licked skin, the hands that grip the side of the boat and expose knuckles raw and white.

Cholly Wong, one suspender hanging off a bony shoulder, knees splayed, pushes off the pier with the shout:

I'll save you!

His legs hold a strength surprising in so short and old a man, and he leaps out so far that his head knocks against the side of the boat. The women gasp as the boat rocks and threatens to spill them.

Cholly falls deeper and deeper into the ice-cold water. He can see only a few inches in front of him. As he aims for the surface, he feels the swoosh of a body diving toward him, a plunge that causes flurries of bottom sand to erupt. Cholly closes his eyes and feels for air, for the breaking of the surface. The light glimmer across the top of the water dims to darkness.

Cholly reemerges in Manny Chow's arms and the crowd sounds out the first notes of cheer, until they realize that the old man is limp and water streams from his nostrils. Manny struggles to pull Cholly onto the pier.

A few women rush forward to drag his wet body into the sun, to give him the dignity of a dry death. Look at them! a little girl cries.

The women in the boat have now drifted well south of the pier. Manny kicks his way back into the river and grabs on to the back of their boat. He directs it to shore and stops when he hears the grit of sand against the bottom of the boat.

Though soaked, the water running off his body in icicle streams, Manny helps the women from the boat with a graceful hand. The feeling of solid land against their tender feet makes their knees shake.

The dark clouds break apart. The fog sinks into the river. Tunnels of sunlight shine through.

3

IT WAS A momentary shudder in the weather, but it has passed and again the sun blazes down on the water until the refraction of light, the tiny diamond glitters, causes everyone to squint. Richard swipes his hand along the beads of sweat rolling down Poppy's flushed face. He fans her with his hat, then holds it so its shadow protects her. In the commotion on the water, no one has noticed her faint, or even now, her limp body on the wood, the splinters snagging her dress.

She opens her eyes and asks, Did you see it too?

The boat? Runaway singsong girls.

You saw them too? I thought I'd dreamed them.

Richard shakes his head and looks over to the murmuring mass of people who have crowded around Manny and the women. Such naked desire for gossip and tragedy. As if these people were not dressed in their parade-day clothes, but unshod in the dirt paths of a village with nothing else to occupy them. Richard says, I'll help you home.

He pulls Poppy to her feet. The flush has not left her cheeks and she looks like a schoolgirl—eyelashes faintly damp, eyes bright and dark in awakening. There's the patter of feet on the dock and a little girl approaches. She's hot too, twisting in her too-small dress and scratching at her waist.

Manny wants you, she says.

Me? Richard asks.

She nods. Her eyes dance as if she holds a surprise.

I'm coming.

THE LITTLE GIRL leads the way with a brisk walk that barely refrains from skipping. She tips her head up from side to side to make sure everyone sees who leads Richard. And the people step aside; the crowd splits like the wake of a fast boat. As the trio slices their way through the group, a smell grows, unnameable but distinct. Poppy stays at his arm, her face now pale, and she strains in anticipation of something. Somber faces alongside him, Poppy silent, the little girl proud. Even Chloe is there, at the edge of the group with her whole dress damp and her balled-up stockings held in one hand. Their eyes meet for a moment before she looks away. Richard feels as if they are all witnesses to his own funeral. Maybe he is already a ghost.

But the real ghost stands at the center, next to Manny. A faded, older version of Richard's wife Ming Wai, whom he has not seen in ten years. She lives in China; this he is sure of, because he sends her money each month, and sometimes a letter as well. She would have no reason to be vengeful and, beyond this, no reason to be here, standing next to Manny, torn-up-looking and smelling like a dead dog. But she has Ming Wai's light-eating eyes, and her pout, and the woman falls to her knees and says, Husband.

She is battered, no doubt. Skin the color of a fading bruise, blues pushing through yellow. Her clothes seem to consist wholly of frayed thread; the tears and splits reveal the pale skin beneath. Her small bound feet peek out from under the hem of her pants. The soles of her slippers have split down the middle from the swell of her feet. She holds out her hands before her and they are brown from the sun. A sharp line at her wrist demarcates where the cloth protected her. Her hair falls from her shoulders in snags, knotted like lost nets at the bottom of the sea.

Husband, she says. Forgive me.

Ming Wai? he asks. He stiffens at the hope heard in his own voice, the falter in two syllables.

I'm sorry, she says. I don't deserve to look at you. The voice makes sense now. It breaks its way across time and his memory. It is Ming Wai. He has always recalled her singing. While she embroidered, she sang the tale of the Weaving Maiden and Ox Herd. Two lovers permitted to marry, then torn apart as punishment for neglecting their work—the shuttle that lay still at the loom and the oxen that trampled the fields. A river of stars separated them, and they were permitted to meet on only one night a year—the seventh day of the seventh lunar month. A flock of birds became a bridge for the two across a wide swath of the night sky.

Richard looks at the two other women who cling together behind Ming Wai—in just as rough a state and of indecipherable ages—then around at the faces surrounding them—the interested ones who can understand; the more interested ones who can't. Delicately furrowed brows that ask: Will he claim her as his wife? Does he even know her? Or is she a long-lost, jilted lover? Poppy has unlinked herself from him and stepped away.

Stand up, he says. Ming Wai moves off her knees to wobble on her pus-and-salt-sore feet. Richard casts off to no one specifically: She's my wife. I'm taking her home. He lets her rest her hand on his arm. Her touch seems unreal, and it's very light—light as a memory, which, for a moment, Richard is sure it is.

HE DOESN'T LET her venture beyond the small kitchen and living room area. He's afraid that beyond that, in the bathroom and bedroom, she will glimpse the life of a bachelor. He seats her at the table that crowds into the kitchen, next to the icebox. He gives her water from the tap; she asks for tea.

I'd hoped our reunion would be more romantic, she says. She touches her torn clothing.

Richard turns to the boiling water. Ten years, he says. I don't understand. I was coming back—didn't you get my telegram?

I paid a smuggler. She runs her fingertips over freckles of salt on the tabletop.

Richard scans her body for signs of violation. She is wind worn, sea worn, sun worn. He realizes he has been breathing cautiously this whole time. As a boy, he'd once come across a dead dog in some tall grass. Flies hummed black around its muzzle as gases wheezed out of the bloated corpse. Richard brings his hand to his nose, looking at his wife and thinking of the dog.

She reaches into her pants pocket and brings out a fold of whisper-thin paper. It is beginning to tear at the creases: Your telegram.

He takes it from her and expects that the words have changed, reconfigured themselves into a call for her to come to America, to risk her life at the hands of a smuggler who packs bodies like cargo for a profit. But the words are the same as the ones he sent across the ocean, though blurred by the oils that creep off fingers. Stay there, wait for me.

Stay there, wait for me, she says, echoing his thoughts.

You disobeyed me, he says, because how can she understand what he gave of himself to give to her? She knows only of the seed money—begged and collected from relatives, taken even from the red envelope money they had received at their wedding. If his father had been alive, he could have found a sponsor. Instead he left against the scorn of his brothers and the shame of his mother. Ming Wai has no idea about his life after becoming a paper son. About his transformation from Fong Man Gum to Richard Fong. In his letters home, he alluded to success, and made no mention of his days toiling away on ranches, working his body like he never had before. He wasn't made for that world—of labor and sun and sweat streaked with soil. The dollar-a-day for split thumbs and itchy pesticide spots on his skin; for the fertilizing, pruning, picking, digging, packing, lifting, and cleaning. All for a suit and some money so he could go with a humble face and broken English to a whiteman and beg for business faith. It will be six more years before he fully owns the gambling hall—even then he can never own the land beneath it.

I'm your wife. You never should have left me. She has become a woman, Richard realizes by the flash in her voice. When he left, she was only eighteen and answered every question with a timid yes or no.

I had no choice. He changes tone. I was working for you, to support you.

The merchants can bring their wives. Li Yin told me. You should have sent for me.

Richard pours water over tea leaves in two cups. The dark green leaves bloom in the water and heat, unfurl like opening hands. He puts the cup before her. When the law had been enacted four years before, a man had committed suicide in front of the American embassy in Japan in protest. For men like Richard, already in America but ineligible for citizenship, it meant no possibility for the immigration of his wife: condemnation to a return or a double life, a family on two shores, or eternal bachelorhood.

I don't own a grocery store, he says. Her hands, which have

leaped for the hot cup, withdraw and she looks up, all around, because (Richard knows she's thinking) she sees that he has failed.

But, he wonders, what about the icebox, the gas stove, electric lights? Water that comes hot from the faucet?

I manage a gambling hall. There are very few wives here. It'll be difficult for you.

I'm not a child and I'm not a whore. There's no work for women here?

You can pack fruit. And there are other things too, I suppose.

I'm not leaving, she says. She sips at the tea, sucking up the liquid between her teeth loudly. Richard looks again at the telegram. It is translucent with spots of oil. She has carried his words across the ocean with her. It has made two trips—one from him to her; another back to him through her. She has arrived with no luggage, mysteriously, and battered. Shipwrecked, or abandoned at the mouth of the Delta waters, but she carried his letter.

She flings the cup at the cabinets. Tea splatters across the wood, a broken wave, and the cup shatters like burst gunpowder.

But it is Richard who begins to cry after the initial startle. She won't look at him. He leaves his chair and kneels in front of her. He opens his mouth and takes in the air that comes from her. She is his wife and he wants it all—the dirt and the odor and the sounds. Her body offended and stiff. He kisses her knees, where the cloth is waxy from weeks of being unwashed, rolls up the legs of her pants, and takes her right foot into his palm.

He begins to catch his breath. He wants to vomit; he wants her to stay. He slips off her split shoes, untucks the end of her cotton binding, and begins to unravel. He frees the toes that press into her arch. He releases the scent of sloughed-off skin—flesh wet with rot from its own humidity. He tips his head and concentrates on the task with lost face. He leaves ten feet of soiled cotton binding in a loose pile beside him, then massages Ming Wai's feet, gently, working blood into her famished limbs. Despite the pain, she is silent.

4

The Sole-Maker's Son (1908)

FONG MAN GUM was enthralled with Lau Sing Yan's tales. Lau Sing Yan had just returned from America—five years abroad. The lot of them gathered at a teahouse to hear his stories. They drank wine and ate and raised their voices to be heard over the din in the place. Now twenty-four and swaggering his adulthood around the younger boys, Lau Sing Yan spat crab shell on the table, and threw emptied clamshells onto the floor by his feet. He finished cup after cup of liquor. Fong Man Gum watched between bites of fish and rice. Lau Sing Yan's face was clean and rosy and impudent, but his nails were dirty.

When it's day here, is it really night there? Siu Baak asked.

Yes. The world is upside down. If you dig deep enough, you'll pop your head up in New York. Lau Sing Yan laughed, nibbled on some fish.

So in America, now it's night?

Yes.

Siu Baak repeated this to Fong Man Gum, though Fong Man Gum had heard every word.

What's America like? another boy asked.

They fear us there, though they'll work us hard. You'll meet all kinds of men. The Irish are the worst of all.

The streets are made of gold? Everyone leaned forward for the answer. Fong Man Gum snickered, but leaned forward also.

Lau Sing Yan laughed. He sucked down two clams before answering with flecks of food on his tongue. No, they're made of stones, like here. The houses are ugly, but inside is furniture made of silk, beds full of feathers.

Fong Man Gum watched two men take a table. They rapped on it. A woman came up to serve tea. One of the men lit a cigarette. He held the cigarette with one hand and, with the other, stroked the back of her thigh. She said nothing. Fong Man Gum cringed at her badly bound feet.

And what about the women? he asked.

The women are easier. You can even marry a whitewoman in some places.

But are they beautiful? someone across the table said.

Not often enough. Spotted skin, big noses. Lau Sing Yan motioned a large nose with his hand.

Okay for a night, if you keep your eyes closed, right?

Everyone smiled, and Lau Sing Yan answered, Exactly.

Siu Baak, in his nervous, breathless way, asked, So, when it is winter here, it's summer there?

In San Francisco, it is nearly always spring. Lau Sing Yan held out his cup. Siu Baak poured more wine from the clay jug.

May you dry your cup, Lau Sing Yan toasted. Fong Man Gum gulped down the strong wine. It was dry and hot and bitter. He felt it all the way down. His head went dizzy a moment later. He tipped his face up, stared at the exposed beams, then squeezed his eyes shut as he tried to erase the taste on his tongue.

The men ate again with a clatter of chopsticks hitting the bowls. Heads tipped in, occasional turns to the side to spit bones and inedible bits on the floor.

Fong Man Gum worked some phlegm up and hocked it onto the floor.

Wine too much for you? Lau Sing Yan asked.

No. You're not the only one who's gotten older, Fong Man Gum said. What do you do with your queue?

Put it up in a hat. It's a good fashion. Cooler on the neck. More wine?

Fong Man Gum shook his head. He glanced at the two men, now joking with the woman as she provided a light for their pipes. She smiled, very quickly, then looked serious again. The girl Fong Man Gum was to marry was still eight years old—ten years younger than he was. He'd gotten some fumbling experience from other girls his age, but nothing that would give him the cockiness of Lau Sing Yan.

Lau Sing Yan held out two strings of cash and called for more wine.

So you have come back rich, Fong Man Gum said, flicking at the strings so that they swung off Lau Sing Yan's fingers.

Richer than you'd ever imagine.

Richer than my father?

With the world hot and wavy, such challenges of ego seemed

funny to Fong Man Gum. He smiled. He glanced around the table. Most were still eating, chatting to each other, but Siu Baak watched anxiously.

Lau Sing Yan stiffened. Not yet. But I will be. He turned abruptly, calling out again for more wine.

Fong Man Gum smirked at the table. His father manufactured rubber soles, sold to America to be made into complete shoes of many styles. He'd built a big house, had a dozen servants. So you can work for the West there or here. Either way, you get rich. I'll certainly drink to that. He tipped his cup for the few drops that rolled down.

While it's true that one can make a fortune here, your father's house is a hovel compared to the homes there. This is what I'll drink to. Lau Sing Yan took the new jug of wine and poured so quickly that it sloshed over the edges. He stood up, held out his cup to Fong Man Gum in a gesture of respect. I drink to Fong Man Gum, who declares that he'll build streets of gold for America with his own money and his own hands. The whole teahouse laughed and drank. Fong Man Gum rolled his empty cup in his hand. He glared over the table, and at the women at the edges of the room who giggled with hands over their mouths. Whores. And Lau Sing Yan with his silky queue and his well-fed body, stuffed full of American food and washed with American soaps and water—he was just some two-bit laborer posturing as aristocracy, hiding his callused hands with careful gestures.

Fong Man Gum stood. The teahouse shifted down to

murmurs. I appreciate your toast; unfortunately, it's late. As he walked away, the room burst into noise.

ON HIS WAY home, Fong Man Gum passed a small pagoda-shaped gambling parlor situated between the facing courtyards of two homes. The parlor called forth its song of glass and ivory and chairs and people day and night. Mostly male voices, but often a woman's voice rose in flirtation or bawdy laughter above the rest. A woman sitting on the arm of a chair, skirt hitched up her thigh, holding smokes and a drink for her man. She was tough, and she had the scars to prove it. The gnarled ear, where a lover, drunk and angry, slammed a chair against her head, rendering her forever half deaf; the chipped tooth; the callused hands.

He twisted his hands and paced by.

He walked into an alley that ran between two stores. Behind the apothecary shop to his right was a dark hut filled with cackling hens. Hot, feathered bodies pressed against the fenced entrance. The smell of shit and feathers and broken eggs gone rancid in the heat arose. He held his breath. He headed away from home as he thought about the prospect of America. It seemed everyone had a cousin who'd gone over to labor. Half had come back. Most men went with no illusions about gold mountains or milk and honey. Hard work was hard work, but over there, your hour, your life, was worth more in paper and coins. Half of what Lau Sing Yan said was a lie—he could sense that. However, all that wealth. More than his father had. This was what intrigued him. But his role was to take over the factory. It was for the younger brother, not the oldest, to set off for the United States.

He continued on a dirt path that bordered watery fields until he reached an incline littered with a collection of buildings. They huddled, brushing crumbled shoulders. Ruts marked the paths winding among them, some so deep they still held water from the last rain. He passed a pigsty roofed with dark rubber marked with the imprint of soles. Scraps from his father's factory. The wealth trickled down through the village—discards used as building and farming materials, markers of property division, roofing, pond floaters. Everyone was a serf to his father, including himself. Against the side of one home: piles of soles and scraps. Chickens rooted among them. He stamped his feet at them; they clucked and fluttered and settled again. Chickens didn't clutter the streets of America.

He wound his way back home. The warmth of a lantern still burned inside some places. His father's courtyard was large. Small maples grew in the corners. He swung open the door to the cool, European-style home. Two stories, many wide windows. His hand glided up the banister as he headed to his room. All the signs of modernization, but he knew that his father's tiled atrium, the stereoscope, the telephone, the Bible, were just Western surfaces. He wanted to remake himself all the way to the core.

5

OUT OF THE dull, quiet afternoon, a gift. The two women, newly arrived and handed over to a strange whitewoman, give her an even stare. A crowd fans out behind them, a congregation of sweating statues in the post-noon sun. Corlissa feels as she did going from door to door in Chinatown, easing her way in with gifts of food, or even a new icebox, to share the Lord. For the Church, feigning submission, with an undercurrent of authority.

So can you? Manny asks.

Howar is not home, but Corlissa has been a preacher's wife long enough. She puts on her bright middle-class smile. One of the women, her fingernails edged with dirt, pulls at the hem of her salt-stiff shirt. A steadiness radiates from each of them—a conscious not-fixing of the hair, not-rubbing at the cheek in a nervous check for dirt. They smell of pressed earth, flowering fennel rolled between fingertips. Despite the women's dulled looks, they spark brightness in Corlissa's bored mind.

Of course. Come in. Corlissa shuts the door to the wondering crowd.

. . .

IN THE ICEBOX there is a fish, a bowl of peas covered with a dishcloth, carrots with dirt-flecked leaves, half a roast caked in cooled grease. Tomatoes in a basket, and pears too. There should be food before bathing, but embarrassment spreads from Corlissa to Manny to the women and soon everyone shifts in response to the odor of humanity so blatantly displayed.

Corlissa shoots small smiles to the women as she and Manny discuss the living arrangement. There must be an end to the shifting, the thin smiles and exchanged glances of introduction. She tells him that they can sleep in the church. It's warm enough this time of year, comfortable with a few blankets laid out. Manny clears his throat. Corlissa rises from under the unspoken that causes tears of embarrassment in the women's eyes.

Perhaps the last thing they want to do is sit in water, she says, but I can ready a hot bath and get them dresses. Manny nods and translates and Corlissa leads the group down a short hall to the bathroom. Manny looks at the ground, shrugs his shoulder against his cheek, and says, I should be going now. Nothing to say between the three women, they watch him go, then Corlissa turns to the bath.

When her hand touches the faucet—hot hand to cold metal—she is sharply aware of the wealth implied in the gesture. Water pours forth like jewels. She wants to explain that the enameled, claw-foot tub with brass fixtures is the result of a wedding night promise made sixteen years before. That she had once lived in a two-room apartment in Chinatown with a shared hall bath and that for the first three years, only cold water came from the tap, and the bathwater had to be shared. Instead, she reaches into the stream and tests the temperature.

Awkward silence as they wait for the tub to fill. She has never seen skin so pale. They are so pale, they seem to vibrate blue, as if the cold of the sea hasn't left them yet. Except for their hands, burnt and chapped. How did they protect their faces? she wonders. Their cheeks are free of any flush at all, sun- or heart-induced. They are not yet ready to smile either. They watch her movements carefully—the stretch of her hand to the faucet, how she wipes her fingertips on her dress. One is still a teenager, nineteen or so, face built so that a smile might transform it from cradle-fresh to fat-cheeked jolly. She clings to the older one, who is bony and tall.

Manny had said the younger is named Sai Fung and the older So Wai. So Wai, Manny solemnly reported, is looking for her husband, employed somewhere in the Delta. Sai Fung seems to have drifted in on the same intention as many others, propelled by rumor and ignorance and will. Etiquette keeps Corlissa from asking all these things: their names, ages, reasons. Instead, excusing herself in her stilted Chinese, she goes to get some towels. The walls are damp to the touch. The women are so weary they don't blink an eye at the familiar language coming from the strange mouth.

SHE TAKES TOWELS from the hall closet, then rummages, with the familiar rattle of mothballs, through her bureau for old dresses. The clothes let up the smell of closed boxes breathing heat and crumpled tissue paper.

She wants to give them old dresses, but not so old that the women feel they are not worthy of something better. She pulls free a dress with a collar made of lace that has stretched. And here is the one with the buttons that droop down the bodice on thread anchors. The worn cloth and faded print remind her of a day at the beach when Sofia was ten. The day of the fire in the East Bay, when curls of burnt wallpaper floated across the bay and landed on the wet sand, the day Sofia nearly drowned, knocked off a rock by a wave. Sai Fung and So Wai won't think of the ocean, or the play of fire versus water, but of their first day in Locke.

Back down the hall. She pushes open the door, excuses herself, and sets the clothes and towels on the lid of the toilet. Their quiet talking stops, but it is the conversation, not the silence, that excludes her. The intimacy of the breaks, the simultaneous intuition toward silence. Sai Fung sits on the side of the tub and smiles.

I'll be in the kitchen. If you need me, Corlissa says.

When she leaves again, she expects the rustle of voices to begin anew, but hears splashing instead.

AS CORLISSA FOLDS a crust over a vegetable and meat pie, Sofia bursts into the kitchen.

Who are they? said breathlessly, a braid coming unraveled. She carries a river stink into the room.

Corlissa wipes her hands and turns toward her daughter. She laces a mass of Sofia's unkempt reddish brown hair between her fingers and sniffs. You stink, she declares. They're in the bath, but maybe you should follow them. Where have you been?

Sofia shrugs herself away. I saw them come in. They were so beautiful. They were so beautiful, Mama. She leans back against the sink, right foot riding up and down her left calf, a soft toe-scratch at an old mosquito bite. I can't wait to meet them.

Where have you been? Corlissa turns back to dinner. Indifference may coax forth the truth.

Sofia picks at carrot bits left on the chopping board: The parade. Then I saw the boats. And the women. Annoyance lightens Sofia's tone, but doesn't settle Corlissa's suspicion.

Let them be. They've come a long way. Get cleaned up. Corlissa opens the oven door and slips the pie in. The black grease burning off the bottom of the oven stings her nostrils. By the time the oven door groans closed, Sofia has already left the kitchen with light steps.

Corlissa can step softly too. She follows her daughter, into the hallway, where one can already hear the splash of water. The air is heavy here, humid; the steam uncurls from under the door and weighs down the hall. The door is cracked a bit and Sofia pauses before it. Over her head, a slim rectangle of view: bodies bending, water poured. A watercolor of pale women bathing, concentrating on the task. A stifled sob sounds, a cry of pure relief. Sofia rebraids her hair as she watches, glances over her shoulder to see if she is caught, and she is caught. Any explanation sits heavy on the tongue. She glances down, then turns away and runs up the stairs.

DINNER ELICITED NO more from them. Sofia was overly helpful and her eagerness made the women draw back. They passed whispers back and forth between each other, even as Corlissa spoke with Howar about the day, and the couple made allowances for their new guests' breaches.

Corlissa sits with her mending on a chair under the light-cone of a floor lamp. She licks the frayed end of thread and tries to guide it through the needle's eye. The thread hits the needle and curves back. Corlissa licks and tries again. She holds the needle higher, in the light, before her eye. The room funnels through the needle's frame. Here is Sai Fung, wandering from sideboard to coffee table, touching everything. Here is So Wai, studying a map of the Delta that Howar has laid out for her. Sofia on the floor, flipping through a magazine and playing with her hair. Howar writes at his desk, pen moving from red-marked Bible to letter paper. Their marriage hasn't seemed to draw any curiosity from the women. Perhaps miscegenation is looped into their myths of America, along with the infamous streets of gold. She could explain the lashings of Chinaman! shouted by her mother, the trip to Nevada, the nearest state where it was legal, for their wedding. But no one in this room cares. She splits the frame with the thread. Her hopes for the day, brought along by these new women, are dissolved by the quotidian.

6

The Flat in the City (1913)

CORLISSA SLID HER fingernail along the spine, shifted it under, and cracked off the shell. Her hands were fast, and the sound of breaking shrimp shells bounced between her and her mother-in-law in the small kitchen. The room was taken up with the smell—shrimp, gray, ready for shelling and more than ready for drying. The two of them had twenty-five more pounds to get through by nightfall and the odor, along with the spattered-grease scent from the speckled walls, was making Corlissa sick.

Sofia, seven months old and squirming, was tied in her lap. She ran her baby hands through the shells and smashed them in her tiny fists. Corlissa dropped another nude shrimp onto the pile and grabbed at Sofia's hands. No, no, baby, she said and slid Sofia's arms back off the table.

Again the motion. The fingernail with the sore skin beneath. This time she tore off the legs and slipped off the shells from there. Water flooded under her nail and the broken shell was sharp against her skin. The shells in one pile, the shrimp in another.

Sofia turned her head toward Corlissa's breast and nuzzled her blouse.

She's hungry, Corlissa's mother-in-law said.

She's always hungry. I'll get her some sugar water.

Corlissa went to the stove, holding Sofia, to dissolve some sugar into water. A sad afternoon light fell through the small window that was partially blocked by a shelf. It was the light of clouds turned cream color by the sun; neither brightness nor grayness. Corlissa heard Ma behind her.

Sugar water. Sugar water for a baby, Ma said to herself.

Sofia's heels pressed into Corlissa's side and she began to make whimpering hunger sounds. Corlissa hushed her, stirred at the pan, then reached for a bottle of Chinese white liquor. She uncapped it, dribbled a bit on her finger, and rubbed it against Sofia's gums.

Small bubbles formed on the bottom of the pan. Corlissa removed it from the heat.

Too much sugar's no good for the baby, Ma said.

Corlissa said, She's teething. It hurts me. She took a rag, knotted the end, and stuck it in the water. The hot sticky water crept up the cloth and turned it dark. She tried to put the knot in Sofia's mouth, but Sofia turned her head from right to left and back, whining and refusing.

See? The baby knows; why doesn't the mother? Ma did not break her shelling pace.

Hush, hush, come on, So. Come now.

Sofia pressed her face against Corlissa's shirt again, against

Corlissa's sore breast, the nipples ringed with small imprints, and moved her head back and forth.

Corlissa sat back down at the table and tried again to give Sofia the sweetened rag. The light seemed to be rapidly falling; night was coming and the shrimp waited in a darkening pile.

She wants her mother's milk.

Corlissa eased her finger between Sofia's lips and gently pried her mouth open. Sofia, Sofia, she sang, Mama has to work.

Ma clicked her tongue.

Corlissa readjusted the strip of cloth that held Sofia to her body. Sofia's body pressed against Corlissa's heart and there was heat where their bodies touched.

The shrimp, the shrimp, Ma said.

Corlissa flared her nostrils, holding back sighs. She wanted to shake Sofia, she wanted to shake Ma, and she wanted to stop shelling. She set the rag on the table in a puddle of melted ice and shrimp juice. You'll just have to cry, she said to Sofia. Sofia's hands curled into fists and she grabbed and pulled at Corlissa.

Ma stood up to light the lantern. The glow and the flicker created long shadows and made the corners darker. They heard the phoomp of the gaslights coming up in the streets.

Howar says in China, the mothers give their babies sugar-cane to suck on, Corlissa said.

I never did. You look at my son's teeth—they are straight. Not rotted. I fed him with my breast until I had his brother. You must be faster.

Corlissa fell back into the rhythm of nail against shrimp. This was how they made their money—two women, day after day, shelling shrimp, so Howar could work for the Church for so little money. He'd rather give up part of his wages to buy Bibles to hand out to the people he greeted in their homes. When the traffic paused for a moment, the sounds of the apartments around Corlissa and Ma rose up—the buzz of sewing machines and other rustlings of work by the women who stayed in to earn their money.

Sofia began to cry. Corlissa jiggled her knee, hummed as she shelled. There was no time to pause—the sun would be down soon and a man would knock at their door to collect their work. Ma shook her head. Corlissa noticed her hair was starting to gray and her shoulders slumped. Ma could do only table work for long periods, and shuffled in small places. Her feet were the size and look of Corlissa's hand when the fingers curled against the palm. Despite the weakness in the feet and the shoulders, Ma's face was shaped and tight, and she disapproved of Corlissa at every turn. Corlissa believed it came to this: she was white, and all that entailed. That the ways she had learned to be a daughter were not how she should be as a daughter-in-law.

Sofia kicked, feet against her mother's stomach, and tented out the cloth that held her. Her wails elevated to screams and Corlissa tried to hunch over the baby's movement, tried to keep working. She blushed.

Go, go, go. Take her away, Ma said.

The shrimp, Corlissa said.

I don't like the noise. Ma's fingers moved faster in response to Corlissa's slack.

Corlissa left the table and slipped into her and Howar's bedroom. She put one hand on Sofia's back and one to her own eyes. Her hand carried the smell of the kitchen and her fingers were puckered with moisture. She began to cry a little. She untied Sofia and laid her on the bed. Then she unbuttoned her blouse. Sofia's chest heaved under its tiny, thin shirt.

Corlissa lay down beside Sofia and brought her to her breast. They curled together, baby inside the curve of mother's body.

7

CHLOE SITS ON the back stoop of the brothel wishing that she had kept some of the tobacco she'd bought for Sofia so she could smoke. She thinks about that afternoon: She's been saved. She undoes one more button on her shirt, fans herself with her hand. If she walks to the front of the brothel, she can look across to Richard's. His apartment is in the back, but maybe she can see the glow of the window against the building next to it. She tries not to look. She runs her heels over the gravel surrounding the stoop. She's been saved; she feels it as real as if it had happened in church—Sofia holding her down until her lungs felt sunk in, so empty of air they stung, and through the water, a blurry Sofia above her, her mouth moving softly and blessing Chloe. It was true—even when she arose out of the water with small river plants clinging to her, and her hair already beginning to smell in the sun, she felt reborn. She was washed of that morning with Richard, and the four hundred nights before that. Even so, she had descended the stairs, turned the brass knob, and sat on the step to wait for their ten-thirty appointment.

George opens the door and looks startled to see her.

I-I-I was going to let some air in, he stutters. He rubs his tattooed arms. His girth and painted arms are intimidating, but his stutter and awkwardness diminish him. As the male presence at the brothel, the protector, it serves him best not to speak often.

I was just getting some air myself. Chloe scoots over. You want to sit?

George eases himself next to her, tugging at the knees of his pants as he lowers himself. He leans against the doorframe and closes his eyes. The tattoos of his right arm, the arm closest to Chloe, are of foxes and fairies and women who dissipate into coiled clouds. Each roll of the clouds is outlined in black that blends into the lines of the women's robes and loose sleeves. The years have bled the ink, which gives the tattoos an even dreamier aspect.

I-I-I heard R-Richard's wife came t-today, George says. His eyes are still closed.

I saw her. A shadow sweeps over them. Chloe looks up at the mist that passes over the moon and then they are lit again.

She's p-pretty. A classic b-b-beauty.

She's all right. She stunk to high heaven. I had to cover my mouth to keep from retching.

He's very l-lucky to have his wife here.

He was doing fine without her.

It sounds like jealousy to Chloe's own ears—she reminds herself that she doesn't like Richard—she hates the curve of his shoulders and the sound of him against her ear. You're right. He is lucky. Chloe turns west. The river is not a hundred feet away, yet she can't hear it. Distantly, there is a train. Nothing else. Two streets in a small town—all silent.

S-So maybe he w-won't come tonight. George stutters his quiet suggestion, but Chloe anticipates the sentence from the first, and each stop and start increases her anxiety and embarrassment.

I know, she says. It was hot. I came for air. It's hot in the attic. Above them, bats shudder against the wall, spin, and flutter back into the night.

George grunts.

Chloe leans her cheek into her hand and smells the river still on her skin. She sighs.

Go sleep, George says. He opens his eyes and lifts his head from the frame. I'll b-bring a fan for you.

Chloe shakes her head. She stands and taps the dirt off her feet, each heel against the lip of the step. I'm going to sleep in the red room.

MADAM SEE RESERVES one room in the brothel for an oil-soaked wick sputtering behind glass. The light shimmers off the red walls and glows through the pink curtains. It is just enough to illuminate the slim bed, to cast shadows on faces and create half-lidded illusions of desire. It smooths out complexions and bestows youth. Chloe lights the lamp and turns back the covers. She crawls in with her dusty pants and sweaty shirt, slides her arms beneath the pillow where the sheets are still cool. She presses her face into the scent of laundry flakes. Nothing remains of the morning—no smell, no coat on the back of the door or stocking flung across the chair arm. Not even the light is the same.

Chloe thinks of how she arrived—on a riverboat to Sacramento, after the pain became too great. The baby was falling and blood was sticky on her thighs. The boat was making a special stop for a troupe of Chinese performers and Chloe hurried off behind them.

One man, with a soft, feminine face, gave her a haughty backward glance. She muttered an apology, but clung to the group as they crossed the road into a town. She recognized it immediately. Locke. The Chinamen's town. She slowed her step. The performers moved on. She considered going to Walnut Grove, but pain sent her scurrying down the sloped road onto Main Street, where she stopped a woman and asked where she could go.

Chloe meant a doctor or a midwife; she felt that the hand low on her pregnant stomach implied this. But the woman couldn't see the spots of blood or the shudder of cramps; she saw Chloe only as a whitegirl. Whitegirls, she'd said, go to Madam See's.

Chloe gave birth in the kitchen. The baby slid into Madam See's hands with slick gray skin and its umbilical cord wrapped tight around its neck like a vine that chokes its own flower.

It's dead, Chloe said. She began to cry and collapsed onto the floor, onto her dress, seeming not to care if it became matted with blood. Richard had been there, in the kitchen. He'd stroked her hair. I was going to keep it, she said. I was going to keep it. He told me to give it away but I was going to keep it.

In response to Chloe's sobs, Madam See urged her to stay the night. Stay a few days. I'll take care of you and in a few days, we'll see what we can do with you.

They burned the baby with the rubbish, and a few days became a year.

She rises to blow out the lamp, but the thought of waking alone in the room at dawn stops her.

POPPY HAD SEEN her picture before, had glanced over Richard's shoulder as he read letters from home, but she was unprepared for the flesh-and-blood sight of Ming Wai standing before her with vixen face and tiny pawlike feet. The tightening around her heart was stronger than on the afternoon when Chloe arrived, when being nearly thirty-two could not compare to a sixteen-year-old with a pregnant belly and a glistening face, and she glanced over at Richard coaxing the girl, touching the back of her neck, unflinching at the blood of Chloe giving birth, and knew in an instant that she'd lost him.

The year Chloe was born, Poppy was standing in the port, newly arrived, fifteen and waiting to meet her husband. A year later, she was traveling as part of an exotic menagerie. Hiding away money for years until she and George ran away and started the brothel in Locke. And it was Richard, a gambling hall manager—not even an owner!—who had made her consider selling the building and leaving it for a more domestic life.

For a whole month after Chloe's arrival, Poppy had left the bedroom light on to wait for him. Finally, in May, she turned it off and lay in the dark waiting. She fell asleep and rose with the sun that heated her room. Chloe waits now. Poppy hears her creep by to the red room, alone.

Poppy folds the clothes at the foot of her bed, lines up her cosmetics, aimless busy tasks to settle her pleased heart. She smiles to herself because, by eighteen, a girl should have her heart broken, at least once.

RICHARD OPENS THE cupboards and the icebox. He shows Ming Wai how to light the stove, which faucet delivers cold water and which hot. She notes with impatience that there is running water in China too. He shows her how he likes the dishes stacked, the food placed.

In the bedroom, he swings open the wardrobe doors. It is his finest piece of furniture—stained a deep red mahogany, six feet high, with a rod for hanging clothes, and two drawers beneath. A few years before, he had gone with some friends to the junkyard to see what they could salvage and sell for extra cash. Richard found this. It had a broken knob, and the edges were worn so the nude wood beneath was exposed, but he sanded and painted and mended. He shows her how his clothes are hung—the hangers spaced two finger-widths apart from each other, so the cloth of one shirt will not wrinkle the next. Two pairs of shoes, the toes stuffed with balled newspaper to maintain their shape. A piece of cedar carved like a bar of soap lies at the bottom of the wardrobe. That keeps the moths out, Richard says.

Ming Wai nods, then her eyes sweep across the single bed. Is that where we'll sleep?

Richard follows her look to the simple blue-and-white-striped sheets and the lone pillow: I suppose we'll have to squeeze in.

You never expected I'd come, she says simply. She turns back to the wardrobe and runs her fingers along his shirts, drags her fingers down the creases made in his pants as they fold over the hangers. It's as if you don't even need a wife. She hobbles over to the bed and sits down.

Her path is traced with tiny smudges of blood. You're bleeding, Richard says, and he hates himself for feeling more concerned with the wood floors than with Ming Wai's pain. Her shoulders sag and she looks down at her feet.

I can't learn to walk again, she says. I'll have to rebind them. It hurts too much.

You'll look old-fashioned. It's been only a few hours. Give the bones a chance to heal. He wipes at the spots with an old sock.

They are healed. You'll have to break them again if you want me to be modern.

Richard kneels to inspect her folded feet. Her legs are loose and thin emerging from the heavy brown wool of his trousers. While she sat in the water, Richard struggled in the kitchen trying to pound two extra holes into his belt with a knife so that she could cinch the pants around her bony waist.

Let's wait until morning at least.

The clock on the nightstand ticks eleven-twenty-one. Ming Wai takes the rope of wet hair hanging down her back and twists it in her hands. Some of her fingernails appear to have been bitten or torn away. The things they could say are loud in the room—the two of them still overwhelmed at the idea of ten years.

Richard says, Let's go to sleep.

They turn away from each other to undress. Richard glances over his shoulder at Ming Wai's icy-white back woven through by muscles and hunger. He waits until she lies under the covers before turning around and sliding in beside her. Her body is cold. She moves closer to the wall to make room for him.

Good night.

Good night.

Richard turns off the light. The moonlight through the windows casts a blue square on the wall—the shape of the window darkened by the shadowed curves of their bodies. Richard lies with his eyes open. They are both silent. Her hand brushes the small of his back and his body tightens. She slides her hand from his back to his hip.

He turns toward her. She is backlit, her face just a dark shadow. He reaches out to touch her damp hair, to tuck it behind her ears over and over. He strains to hear her breath, but can hear only his heart in his ears. She rolls her hips toward him. This is when the desire should begin, when he should feel a stirring, should do more than twist her hair between his fingers. She kisses him. He tightens his grip on her hair and pulls her head away.

You don't want me, she says.

I want you.

Ten years, she reminds him, and he cannot tell her that it's been ten years for her, but far less for him. He swallows heavily and whispers, I'm sorry. She rolls toward the window. His fingers slide through her hair, down the coarse strands to the very ends—hair so long it touches her elbows—and brings it up to his mouth. Her feet kick him away, but there is nowhere for either to go on the small bed. He chews on her wet hair and thinks of three things at once: the taste of his own hair when he would suck on his queue while bathing as a child; Chloe alone in the red room; the wrenching in Ming Wai's back as she cries—and he wonders how he can balance them all.

8

In the Pear Orchard (1919)

RICHARD ARRIVED IN the summer, one young man among many.

Heat rose. The barracks were stifling when the pear pickers returned in the evening. The heat drove them out—toward town, toward Main Street, toward gambling and women. Main Street was where the Delta breeze swept over the levee and down into town.

Mosquito bites so bad they bruised. He peeled back the bedding and found fleas between it and the mattress. The mattress stained in the shape of a sweaty body. Lice in the pillow.

He kept a locked valise under the bed filled with all that was important—papers, portraits of himself with Ming Wai, a change of clothes. He wore the key on a chain.

With the fifty-pound pear bag slung crosswise across his chest, with his hands reaching to pluck the pears that had not yet turned blush-hued at the bottom, with feet in a constant state of readjusting balance on the ladder, he had never conceived of such weariness. It was more than when they hurried to tie bandannas around their faces as the crop duster's spray drifted into the orchard; more than the ache that spread from wrist to the wings of his back, so that each shift in bed brought new pain. Because there was loneliness too.

He needed to feel his body was real; it had gone without touching for so long. Even a shoulder brush loosened him. He found ways to ease himself.

He shat. He urged it out even when he was not ready, just to feel the functioning of his body. He found that he didn't mind the stink or darkness of the outhouse, nor the newsprint tacked to the wall to wipe with. He wanted it all—the rancid smell, the gassy heat, the slump of his body thrown into the act. The moment of pleasure at release.

He groomed. With a toothpick, he scraped the dirt out from under his nails. He cut his nails, slowly, savoring the shearing away of growth. He plucked at his eyebrows with newly cut fingernails.

And then, finally, there was that of which he would never speak. Near the end of the harvest. Two of them, at the farthest corner of the orchard with no one but the trees around them. They were slow to finish up. Richard stepped off the ladder. One hand trying to stay the falling of pears from the bag, a foot that slipped on the last rung; the sudden warmth of a steadying hand at his back. Richard sank into it. The other man, Ah Lum, maintained his touch. A half glance backward from Richard; understanding transferred in a look. Ah Lum was younger, not older than twenty, but his will was unflinching. Richard turned around and leaned against the ladder.

The work whistle blew. The ladders would be stacked up and the men lined up for food.

Richard closed his eyes. His belt was undone, his button unclasped. The air cool on his unbundled body. He wanted to cry out and say no, but more than that, he wanted someone else to know his body was real too.

First was Ah Lum's hand, then his mouth. Richard gripped the ladder and participated only by his presence. He looked up through the heart-shaped leaves and to the flat blue sky. Bees hummed at the open wound on a yellowed pear. Afterward, Richard knew, he would wish it had been all a dream, or a stumbling midafternoon thought.

He ejaculated onto the grass.

Richard couldn't meet Ah Lum's eyes. He buckled his pants, then pulled the ladder shut. Help me carry this, he said. They marched back to camp. Two men flashing through the trees, ladder held between them, each slung with fifty pounds of pears to weigh them down.

9

THE SUN SETS on the other side of the river. Men leave work by the setting sun and march into Locke, alone and in groups. Their boots have been cleaned of cannery waste, or field dust—shined leather for a Saturday night. They fill up the diners and the gambling halls and the speakeasy—throw their dice, drink their drinks with steady hands, as if the present action is all they have come for. Every opening door causes their heads to turn—just a casual glance backward— an eye seeking out the shape of a woman. They are patient.

The men have come from all over and the boarding-houses are full; there is no place for those from other towns. After dancing, when the sweat has dried, the phonograph shut, the records carefully resleeved, the men suck in their stomachs and squeeze onto the stairs to sleep. Backs against the wall, legs bent up on a short step, or lying full out on the dance floor. So many packed bodies, there is no need for blankets.

They are waiting for Sunday morning. Straws have been drawn and punches thrown over who gets to sit with the boat-women first. The men have scheduled themselves to enter the Lees' house by twos, to take off their hats, sit politely, and smile at the new women they hear have arrived.

But first, there is church. This Sunday it is standing room only. The whole curious town has filled the pews; everyone stares not at the preacher, but at the backs of the two heads in the very front. There is something gauzy and uncertain about the women, as if in a blink they will be gone.

The preacher tells the story of Noah's Ark. It is a story better suited for Sunday school, but he is new, underestimates their Christian educations, and so the congregation forgives him. When he lists the animals, the rhythm of the pairs—elephants, eagles, zebras, tigers, ostriches, horses, lions, doves, ravens, dolphins—lulls the listeners into being five again, or twenty-five, learning the names. Sows, bulls, hens, mares, ganders, toms, and bitches. The men whose backs still hurt from the dancing hall stairs nod in understanding.

Hymnbooks turn into fans. The Jesus hung on the cross on the wall sweats, the wood gaining the luminescence of trees in the rain. Preacher Howar Lee looks down at the red-faced people before him and closes up his sermon. They rise to unstick their legs from their seats.

On the lawn, the men who have waited since sunset of the night before pull themselves together with whispers. They have chosen a representative to talk to the preacher and his wife—to voice their plan to court the boat-women. Fifty-two men vying for the attentions of two women.

. . .

CORLISSA'S VOICE REACHES over the men who stand expectantly on her front porch as she calls her daughter's name.

Sofia!

Sofia rises, breaking through soft white shirts with yellowed stains under the arms, through the heat rising off nervous chests. The men frown as she passes; she has sat among them, silently, without their knowing.

Corlissa reaches out and pulls her daughter forward. Just a moment, she tells the men. Just another moment.

Like animals, she says behind the closed door. They smell like bulls pacing the paddock. She looks Sofia up and down to see what kind of trouble she's drawn.

It's hot inside, Sofia says. So I went out. Words fight against Corlissa's teeth. She licks her lips.

The curtains hang still in the breezeless day and melted water dribbles from inside the icebox and into a metal pan. Get them some water. Keep them calm. I knew they weren't all looking for the Lord.

I'VE ALWAYS WANTED to go to Africa. All that forest unfurling across the continent. The heat. The humidity. As if there wasn't enough of that here.

For sure.

And the river. I always have to be near a river. I get thirsty just thinking about deserts. I come from city people—a great-great uncle of mine was an adviser to the Daoguang emperor.

Sweat darkens the pulled-button shirt splitting across the suitor's stomach. The women sip their tea and politely smile at the eleventh claim of distant royalty that day.

My father is a scholar. He's in San Francisco, but he went back to the village when I was thirteen and they still called him Teacher. He works at a hotel, real nice, looks like the White House. Lucky. The village fortune-teller took my mother aside when she was heavy with me and told her my family's luck would change when I was born. And it was true. Look at me, in America talking to you two lovely women.

The younger one giggles, but the older, aloof one looks away. The man clears his throat.

Um, yes, I hope I can call on you next week. I heard the acrobats are coming to Walnut Grove. Maybe we could try an outing. He stands up and thanks the whitelady, somnolent chaperone, who slouches in a chair, nodding off.

Then the next one. Number forty-nine. The women stop feigning interest. Bulls pacing a paddock, impatient cows kicking away to the pasture.

THE DAMN GIRL! Corlissa had been in the kitchen with her for an hour, washing all those glasses. Away for ten minutes and Sofia has slipped out already. The kitchen is full of the red light of the setting sun. Corlissa takes up the rest of the washing. Pinches of anger tighten on her neck and face. The scroop of the back door opening.

You didn't finish washing, Corlissa says.

I just stepped out for a minute.

What did you do? Sofia stands in the doorway, two limp braids in one hand and grease-sticky kitchen scissors in the other. A tiny shake in her hand as she stares at her mother. Her hair is jagged past her ears in an uneven bob like a flapper or a theater woman. Corlissa shakes the soap from her hands and walks over to take the braids. What did you do? Her fingers brush Sofia's lobes where the hair ends. You look like trash.

What's done is done, Sofia says. It was hot on my neck.

It's really awful.

It's done. She's impatient with her mother's surprise.

Corlissa shakes her head.

Unbelievable. She dangles the braids. You were going to keep these?

I guess.

No.

I was going to keep them. She makes a reach, but Corlissa won't let go.

You're going to come with me. What kind of daughter?

Corlissa grabs Sofia's arm and leads her to the incinerator behind town. The length of the hair is irrelevant; it's the impertinent lip, the unashamed stare that leads her to the garbage piling up among the weeds with her fingers bruising her daughter's arm. Things too unimportant to be burned, forgotten outside the incinerator's metal mouth: old dolls, papers, potato peelings and sodden apple cores, boxes, torn blankets and a single red woman's shoe.

No, Mama, Sofia cries.

Corlissa opens the door. A whoomp of heat, distorted mirage light wavers out and dries their mouths and eyes.

I want to keep them.

Throw them in. She hands the braids to Sofia. It is the battle itself that matters. Sofia wavers. Corlissa grabs her wrists and thrusts them toward the fire. Drop them! Her knuckles are burning. Sofia starts to howl and pull away. Corlissa is stronger. She yanks to Sofia's pulls, a tug-of-war until the braids are dropped and both are sickened by the smell of burned hair. Sofia rubs at her raw wrists and cries all the way home.

HOWAR IS AGITATED. He kicks his feet, pulls at the sheets, then wriggles them off again. Every movement jars Corlissa awake. She sighs alongside him, impatient, until finally she slips from bed, puts on her dressing gown, loops the belt in a double knot and leaves the room. She paces the hall, remembers the back-and-forth in bare feet with Sofia in her arms. She stands outside Sofia's door. She pauses with her hand on the knob, then opens the door; Sofia is asleep. What did she expect? Sofia looks much younger in the dark room, and Corlissa almost wants to wake her, just so she can soothe her back to sleep. Instead, she listens to her breathing, then steps out and goes downstairs.

Maybe warm milk will make her sleepy. She turns on the kitchen light. The pots clang and echo. There is nothing more lonely than an empty, lit kitchen at two in the morning. She heats the milk, stirring slowly, feeling the spoon catch on the scalded bits on the bottom of the pan. She turns at the sound of a moth beating against the kitchen light. When the gas sputters off, and she stands next to the stove drinking her milk, there is no sound at all, except for the light scuffing she makes in her robe. The wallpaper she hung around the kitchen border last week isn't exactly straight. Geese led with a blue ribbon by a girl, around and around the room. She'd balanced for hours on a kitchen chair, arms in the air, glue dripping off the brush.

She wipes the milk from her lip and puts the pan in the sink. The curtains flutter. Maybe a walk will tire her out. In the living room, the moon reveals streaks on the floor. The men had left footprints. One hundred and four feet going from door to sofa. She had scrubbed and scrubbed, but she sees on the edges residual prints, dust and grass marks. She spits on the corner of her robe and rubs away at the floor.

She'll come back in the morning. All those men lining up just to woo two women—one married, even!—in five minutes of storytelling. It had been easier with Howar. The church had brought them together. It still surprises her, that she has married a Chinese, but it has ceased being strange.

She goes outside, around to the attached church. Inside, the women sleep on the floor. As excited as she is by her new guests, they are still unknown, and she prefers they don't sleep in her house. They say they're not runaways, but to show up like that—no doubt they're illegal. Howar wanted Sofia to give up her room, but Corlissa gathered up the pillows and blankets and walked out to the church. It was done.

Peeking in windows, drinking milk—these do not solve her restlessness. She turns away from the church and slides between houses, each with its lights off. The cats scurry away, and she hears a dog bark on the other side of a wall. Somebody yells for it to shut up.

Walking between buildings so short she can still see the sky, Corlissa forgets to miss San Francisco. So used to the city lights reflecting back orange off the night fog, she had forgotten stars. Locke. A man's town. The cruelty of laws has twisted the place into a Wild West throwback, where men outnumber the women twenty to one. Despite her own marriage, she still feels a distaste rising up at the unusual coupling of white prostitutes and Chinese men. Aberration added on to vice. Yet this is a place where Howar thrives, more work than they'd imagined, and side money too—paid off by brothels and gambling halls to focus on other sins. Howar calls it tact.

After the fish market, she turns left onto Main Street. She'd been taken on this tour when she visited last year, still debating the move. Now every idiosyncrasy is familiar. Across the street is the rooming house; inside the beds are set out in rows. An old widow, Mrs. Sin, runs it, and charges two dollars and fifty cents for a week of meals. Even her age and growing dementia do not keep her from being the regular recipient of marriage proposals. Next door, the Wah Lee and Co. Boots and Dry Goods store, specializing in handmade boots. The place smells of leather and grease, and Corlissa has stopped buying flour there, convinced the boot smell has crept into the taste. The lights in the apartment above Jack Yang's restaurant are still on. The Main Street restaurant is one of several Yang owns around the Delta. This one does well off business from the Star Theatre next door. They say the theater's seen better years. Even traveling acrobats from China once performed there, but now the entertainment is only as exotic as a vaudeville troupe from San Francisco. Lee Bing's restaurant faces the theater. Despite its reputation for having a wandering ghost, it brings the briskest business. Lee Bing, one of the town founders, is the main reason. Even Howar will choose Lee's place two times out of three, just to stay on his good side. Being located next to the Lucky Fortune also helps. The manager, Richard Fong, has turned the gambling hall into the most successful in town. Corlissa marvels that its dark walls and boarded windows betray nothing of what is inside. If she'd been raised in the Delta, the places and people would radiate histories and private jokes—who almost drowned as a toddler, which man hits his wife, which eternal bachelor lost his shirt to a succubus. Newly arrived, she has only surface details, outlines of power. She knows how the money flows, and to whom. Farther down, she might glance up at the Japanese barber's place, peer through the window at the dried plants and medicines at another of Lee Bing's ventures, the herb counter, or strain for the sound of the dance hall above the ice-cream parlor. Instead, she turns her gaze right, at the two-story building facing the Lucky Fortune. Madam See's brothel, one of many in town. This is where some of the money flows. And some save their vitriol against prostitution for this one house, owned by a Chinese madam. Past Main Street, Locke tries to forget the bachelors crowding the rooming houses. Past Main Street, Locke considers itself a family town. Locke is a Chinese town. Corlissa has learned, through the initial sneers, that it is for the strange and exotic whites to carry the distasteful jobs. Poppy See lowers the dignity of everyone.

But there are lights behind the fluttering yellow curtains. Some laughter. A little noise. She wonders about what goes on in there. Desperate men? Forbidden white girls? She steps a little closer. A small beating distracts her. Above, on the yellow bulb. Moths clustered and fighting toward the diffused glow. Their wings collage over the glass.

The blast of an overnight boat carrying cargo down the river reminds her of the time. She turns down the alley past the Lucky Fortune, the walls that pose as dead shell. Howar taught her a famous couplet about love in the later days of their courtship: A silkworm spins until death; a candle weeps itself dry.

10

CHLOE WAITS UNTIL nightfall to look for Sofia. She waits until the lights go dark up and down the street. She knows who George is sweet on, and they make an exchange: his secret for hers.

Someone walks down the alley ahead of her. She pulls back, leans against the side of the gambling hall, and waits. Things should be quiet by ten. It's rare for her to happen upon another person wandering the alleys. Dead center of the planked alleyway is the quietest.

Before going to Sofia's window, she pauses at the church. She has not seen the boat-women since their arrival. The room exists only in shades of blue and gray. In blue light, the women sprawl on the floor, woven in and out of lumped blankets. They shine with relief and exaltation. No lights are on, but Chloe can see their settled faces, their limp hands. They cast their own blue haze into the dark church, where even Jesus-on-the-cross is in the shadows. Chloe grips the sill and presses closer to the window. They are so close, held away by mere glass. The bubbles in the glass trap the blue light. Runaway prostitutes, some have said. Despite the speculation, they are without pasts or stories. They could be anyone. And here, in Locke, they've found sleeping sanctuary in the church.

She walks around the church and looks up at Sofia's dark window on the second floor. A light shines behind the curtained back-door window, and Chloe glides away to avoid its cast. The yellow house, attached to the church, sits on a circle of lawn that bleeds over into the neighbor's. There is no fence, no front or back. The light switches off. Chloe gives twenty seconds for the person to move from kitchen to bedroom. She imagines running for the door. Knob held tight, turned slow. She presses her body to the door as she pushes it open without a creak. She's never been inside. She imagines dark yellow linoleum floors. Rag drying over the lip of the sink. She drags her fingers across the wall to guide herself through the night-blind hallway. The bump of a light switch. Shape of a door, then free air. The stairs. Above, the challenge will be to find the right bedroom. Will Sofia's door be hung with some plaque? Painted wood with the Lord's Prayer in pretty flower script? Indeed it is. The door isn't latched. A gentle push, and it swings open silently. Sofia is sitting up in bed, blanket pulled up to her chin, waiting for the intruder whom she has sensed for minutes now.

Chloe's fear ends her fantasy. She creeps a little closer, as if sizing up the house, then leans against a tree. The light in the kitchen still shines. Should she wake Sofia? She and Sofia have been sneaking out for a month now, nightgowned and barefoot into the summer nights. Chloe can think of no better relief for the monotony than this scrap of brightness, running around with the wine-haired girl who was the first girl outside the brothel to talk to her. Sofia had sat right next to her, Coke in hand, on the bench outside of the Yuen Chong Market, and asked if Chloe was visiting. She was a half woman in girl's clothes—tanned and freckled, white-socked and dirty-kneed, with a kitten mouth and coffee-colored eyes. Her tantrums made Chloe smile.

She waits for some nudge at the window that will show that Sofia too is waiting, but even after the kitchen light switches off, Sofia's room stays dark.

THE HOWLING OF the coyotes in the pear orchard haunts Chloe's sleep. They race among the pear trees, trample rotting pears, track the sweet juice behind them. She's among them. She runs too, across the acres of pears, across the dirt road that cleaves the orchard. She leaves funnels of dust behind her. When she reaches the post-and-barbed-wire border, she turns back and lopes up the road that leads to the Locke family home. It's built on Indian burial ground. Beneath her paws, the rocky dirt turns to soft dust, fed by blood and bones. She circles the house and sniffs the scent of sleeping people inside. She squeezes beneath the porch, beneath the lattice, and digs. There is her own breath huffing hot in the dark, the whine of her anxiety as her nails scratch at the dirt. She uncovers a tiny skull. She clenches it in her mouth, and eases her way back out from under the house. She runs back down the road and into the trees. The other coyotes follow her. She leads, dizzied by the sound of feet trampling grass behind her.

II

UNDERNEATH RICHARD'S WORDS, Poppy knows there are things unspoken. He wouldn't have come otherwise. Is she pleasing you? When you kiss her, does she wet your lips with her saliva? Does she cry real tears? And when you fuck her...?

But these are questions too intimate to ask. So she tells him the things she knows, the things he doesn't need to tell her. When Richard tells her she is thinking not as a seer, but as a businesswoman, she tells him the problem (the threat, the danger) is more than competition. Richard scoffs. Finally, he sinks into one of the plum velvet chairs and ends the conversation with a dismissive laugh and asks to see Chloe.

After Richard leaves, Poppy sits with her indignation. She does know things. After her arrival in America, she'd befriended a woman from New Orleans who also worked with the singsong girls. The girls sang, danced, and served, and then, when only strong white liquor was left and toasts were done, during the digesting period of nursing drinks, their boss presented Sarah.

He introduced her as a native princess, rubbed her pink nipples with coal, dressed her in long blue feathers and uneven wooden beads, and made her dance around and around the tables. Sarah was his highest-paid dancer, adding exoticism to his already exotic stock with her lemon-green eyes and burnt-butter skin.

Their boss, a whiteman catering to whitemen, advertised Chinese courtesans and a real African princess in posters that ran wild with ink illustrations and swooping letters. The spectacle traveled from city to city, banquet to banquet, the women treated little better than finely dressed whores. And they did not cater only to society's lowest. Some of the richest hired the troupe (the fiction of their title!) as well, and brought their wives, who giggled over snifters of brandy, the lust growing in their pale citified eyes.

The boss narrated a tale about a captured African princess brought before the Emperor of China. Poppy, barely into her twenties, was the Emperor—dressed in royal yellow robes and coiled black hair. She wore a fake mustache and beard, which she twirled between her fingers as she swung her other loose-sleeved arm in passionate exclamations at Sarah. Then he made them do things Poppy had heard about only in whispers about women who loved women. She thought them mythical creatures, these women, like phoenixes, but here was Poppy, her mouth on Sarah's breast, or between her legs, as whitewomen in furs and with corseted breasts gasped in a horror that was excitement.

Later, in a back room off of the kitchen, the women undressed. Sarah wiped the coal from her body and Poppy peeled away her mustache and beard. Sarah accompanied each motion with a sigh until Poppy comforted her with the promise of better things.

How do you know? Sarah asked, and Poppy told her about her premonitions and dreams.

And you can tell my future?

I can try.

Do you need to see my palm?

What for?

To see my future. Can't you read my palm?

Poppy tried to explain that it was more than the creases in one's palm. It was the heat below the skin, the sense of a person through their touch and smell and beyond that, a feeling that could be explained only as faith. Poppy asked for a piece of Sarah's clothing to sleep with. The scent could inspire dreams.

As the caravan traveled through the night, they slept on bunks inside a wagon, Poppy with Sarah's shirt smelling sweet and faintly of mildew beneath her head. She never dreamed the absurd ephemera she'd heard peppered the sleep of others. She distinguished her premonitions from her dreams by the clear logical narratives of the former, no matter how surprising the discovered information.

In her sleep, she saw: Sarah, in her twenties, on a turn through Oakland meets a man, a butcher, with glasses so thick they stretch his eyes to watery lengths. He is a tall and pasty man with jutting shoulders and no upper lip. Yet there is something about him that assures Sarah—a fatherly glance over the counter, the extra strips of bacon or lean meat he slips into her order before he rolls it up in crackling white paper.

Sarah becomes carnivorous, and returns to the butcher's every day, if only for soup bones. She returns for ten minutes of conversation across a glass meat case until he invites her for an evening drive to the hills.

With the lights emanating from the hills to the sea in lines, and San Francisco in the glowing distance, they eat olives and drink homemade wine. (Black market trading, he confides, I traded a lot of beef for this.) She feels his knobby fingers on the back of her neck and is not naive enough to wonder where this leads. She knows, and so she leads, with only a glancing thought to the gold band he wears.

The night on the hill is followed by free cuts of meat: T-bone, pork loin, filet mignon, pig knuckles, rump roast. When she finishes cleaning houses, and he finishes slicing and selling meat, they share the evening.

She knows, she knows he has a wife, but she also knows she deserves this little love he bestows upon her. She can't be blamed if a woman can't keep her own man. And so when he says, Will you marry me? and offers her a tarnished emerald ring, she says yes. They marry at city hall and he kisses her and says he can't bring her home. Not just yet.

Then there is the part that Sarah would not see, but Poppy

did: the butcher's return home to his wife and two sons. The wife, Hannah, is also thin and knobby and older, just like the butcher. Her hair, flat and stick-straight, is nearly all gray and cut into a severe bob. She also works hard, maintaining a home with a small green yard where her boys had played in a tub of cold water during a summer years before. Her two sons hold the promise of good looks lacking in either of their parents.

Childhood sweethearts. It would take a childhood sweetheart, Hannah thinks, to tolerate his idiosyncrasies. The butcher shaves his legs and armpits, and his hands always smell of meat about to turn. She is not so lovesick as to think she loves these things about him, but she tolerates them.

So when he returns home and tells her bluntly that he no longer loves her, she feels she deserves a bit more. But when he tells her he's given her emerald ring to a twenty-five-year-old maid, her heart stops. He watches her blankly as she cries and screams. She lifts a hand at him, which he calmly grabs and holds to her side.

Hannah throws herself on the bed (their bed their bed) and the butcher sits awkwardly beside her. He considers offering her a comforting hand, just a touch on the back, but stops himself. As she drifts off to tear-exhausted sleep, she murmurs, I won't give you a divorce.

To the butcher, this is the most outrageous declaration of the evening. She won't grant him a divorce! He goes to the garage to search for a solution. He finds it in a hammer hanging on the wall. He rushes back to the house to catch Hannah still in sleep. He sees only her back and her head cradled in her crossed arms like a reprimanded child. I won't give you a divorce. The singularity of the statement. What selfishness— to not allow his happiness because of her own unhappiness! After seventeen years of marriage. He swings the hammer and drives it into the back of her skull.

When Sarah awoke and sought out Poppy's revelation— would she leave this troupe, would she marry, would she be rich?—Poppy told her as honestly as she could, You will find true love.

What Poppy would like to tell Richard, as she fumes in the wake of his leaving, is that years after she escaped the traveling show, she opened the *Sacramento Bee* to a picture of Sarah. She was older and wore a large hat. Her head tipped back, her mouth straight and haughty—a face that said, I won the man. And below the picture, the story of a butcher who killed his wife with a hammer for the love of a woman with burnt-butter skin.

RICHARD HAS GONE to the red room again. Even with her hands over her ears, Poppy hears voices. The whole house vibrates with them—not only in that room, but all of the others that line the hall. And even deeper than these, voices of people who came before—no one has died in the house, but echoes remain of words said with passion. Sound waves that endlessly bounce against the walls, trapped. Her senses are getting sharper. As a young woman, she'd been able only to see things. Through her twenties, the other abilities had intensified: now she can hear the people crying out from their graves or back from the future, and can sniff out a person's secrets. She longs to break down Chloe's world with a word to the preacher's wife, but first she must go see Uncle Happy.

EVERY SUNNY DAY, a man squats at the side of the road and writes characters in the dirt. Top to bottom, right to left. The scrape of the stick in the dirt whittles it to a fine point. Children peer around corners and laugh. Poppy passes him on her way to the Men's Center. It is whispered that he suffers from the lack of a wife.

Poppy stands a moment in the doorway of the center to allow her eyes to adjust to the dim light inside. A man sitting on a bench next to the door watches her.

Hey, you old whore! You can't go in there. Men's Center, can't you read?

Poppy spits past his feet and steps into the room. She squints into the darkness. Happy sits near the back, reading the paper. The bench he sits on was carved with dancing dragons and phoenixes by Happy himself and the wood has gone smooth and shiny, the flared scales on the dragons eased and rounded.

She takes the kettle off the warmer and offers him more hot water for his tea. She pours some for herself and joins Happy on his bench.

She takes his hand in hers. He has been thinking of opium,

the occasional ball of it pressed into the bowl of his pipe. His intense desire followed by guilt and an impassioned letter home, yet another for his wife to add to the pile of correspondences from a husband she has not seen since 1866. He cannot even remember her face; the image faded only a few years after his arrival and so he clings to this: the soft rusk of his fingertips across her red silk veil on their wedding night. He hears her giggle, and supposes the presence of his nervous erection. But everything is so long ago, he feels like a split river, a branch far from the confluence and flowing helplessly to sea. Poppy lets go. From her handbag, she pulls a cigarette box and offers it to Happy; he waves his hand. She lights a cigarette.

Uncle Happy, you haven't been in to see us!

I'm too old.

One is never too old.

I can't even pack my own pipe anymore.

We can pack your pipe.

Happy laughs. Seeing one of your girls pack my pipe might give me a heart attack.

Poppy tips her head and gives him a demure look. She takes a drink of tea.

Still having dreams? he asks.

Always.

And what do they say now?

You know the women who came?

Everybody's been talking of them. Talking talking talking—the buzzing in my ear won't stop. They are young? Beautiful? Unmarried? What kind of refugees are they?

One claims to be Fong Man Gum's wife.

And is she?

Yes.

And your dreams?

I think—Poppy taps her nail on her cup—I'm not sure, but I don't think they are who they claim to be.

That sounds like the protest of a jealous woman.

Poppy smiles, relents: Sometimes it's hard to tell when a dream is just that. I mean, I think they are ghosts.

Happy nods as he puts fresh tobacco into his pipe. He says, There are ghosts up and down the Delta. Locke is the least of their hauntings. Ten thousand dead between here and Suisun alone. Ten thousand! Hell, the Locke house itself is built on an Indian burial ground.

These aren't Indian ghosts.

The rippled scratch of a match struck: I saw men go myself. When we were reclaiming the land, we had no place to bury them. We lived in the camps, moving around, so we just stuck them in the ground wherever we were working. Some are in the levees, their bones worked into the peat, into the dirt. I'd imagine many of them are unhappy. Maybe they're looking for me. Happy sucks on his pipe. He rolls the smoke around in his mouth, blows it out. Then, as if remembering China is just one step from remembering building the levees, Happy rubs his scalp and says, You know, my wife is still in Chungshan? Have I told you this? Sixty-two years I haven't seen her.

Yes, Uncle Happy.

Yes, I have told you. But I'm too poor, too old now. He smiles and sighs.

The ghosts, she reminds him.

Every plank of wood—from floor to ceiling—ghosts. Babies, adults, old people. And they've been here longer. My own wife is in Chungshan, you know. Eighty-three years old. No children. Ghost or not, let them be. A man deserves his wife. My own wife—such little feet you could cup in a hand. In just one hand! Tiny, bundled up like small...thrushes. No, sparrows. No. No. Hummingbirds. Like small limp humming-birds. She came from a good family. I ruined her. The money. Everything. What good are those beautiful feet now?

I don't know, Poppy says. She crushes her cigarette on the floor and kicks the crumple of paper and tobacco shreds away. How will I know if it's a premonition or a dream?

Always burn hell money. It never hurts. Like a humming-bird, lying limp in your hand. Your feet—those would be peasant feet back home.

Girls don't bind their feet anymore.

Oh yes, he says in sudden remembrance. The revolution. You know, Sun Yat-sen came to the Delta. I saw the bed he slept in.

You've mentioned that. Poppy takes the tone of a nurse guiding a patient back to bed: Can I get more water for you before I leave?

Oh no, oh no. You just go. He sets his pipe back in his mouth. Poppy rises without a good-bye.

As Poppy walks to the door, she tries to release everything she

has absorbed through Happy's bench. The scatter
most of them relating to money. The money he cou
to go home spent on opium instead. Before he quit
he split his boardinghouse rent—five dollars a month—
another man and they alternated between staying there and
the field barracks. Happy came back on the weekends—a place to
sleep during his stay in town; a place to store his things.

Now the room is his own, and he shores up his walls
with his possessions. Poppy travels with him, stepping into
the small single-bed room, and eases herself through a narrow passageway to the bed. She sucks in her stomach when he
does, shares his conscious moves to not tumble the stacks of
old newspapers, empty jars, carefully folded rice sacks, three
deflated bicycle tires (that surely can be mended), one bicycle handlebar, an electric fan (that snaps when plugged in but
does not rotate), a gutted radio, four tin plates (one with a
punctured bottom as if fork tines have pressed through), a jar
of wooden chopsticks (tips singed from cooking), and a spoon
of cheap metal bent awkwardly on its handle. All else Happy
has forgotten, lost track of.

Inside Happy's mind, inside this room, Poppy is held in
by these four walls of things—things that can be used and
improved upon. Things that can be touched.

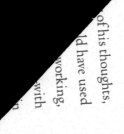

of his thoughts,
ld have used
working,
with

ımmingbird (1865)

THE SOFT RUSK of fingertips on a red-silk veil.

He brought his finger to his mouth and bit. She giggled behind the fabric.

Are you afraid? She asked. She was seventeen and bold.

No, he said. He was eager. So eager, it made him afraid and his thighs quivered and his arms shook. The baubles and silver of her headdress tinkled. She took his hands and brought them to the edge of her veil.

Lift, she ordered. Lift, or I'll do it myself.

He lifted up the whole headdress, careful not to knock off the glass beads. He kept his eyes on it as he set it down. He wanted to extend for a moment longer the anticipation of seeing her.

She was pale and small-featured; her eyes, nose, and mouth gathered in the center of her face. A scatter of pimples on her temple. She smiled at him with small teeth centered in a red-heart mouth.

You look so afraid! She placed her hand on his cheek.

I'm not afraid, he claimed. He scratched at the light stubble

on his chin. He had never kissed a girl. He breathed and con-
centrated on the smoky smell of the banquet still in his nostrils. She closed her eyes and pressed her lips to his. He moved
his lips against hers, finding movement, rhythm, lips, tongue.
He mingled the taste in his mouth with the waxy taste of her
lip color. Her fingers fluttered at the frogs on his shirt and she
pulled it back. He was bare skin to the waist. He pushed at her
dress until it too fell away.

Outside the window, groaning noises erupted, followed
by laughter. Wedding night initiation from his friends. He
raised his head in pause, and she gazed up at him, bare of lip
color and panting. He went to the window and shouted good-
natured threats at his friends until he heard the fading patter
of their feet and laughter. He looked at her from the window:
her persimmon-colored nipples and the goose pimples that
broke across her flesh.

He sat on the bed again. She sat up and brought her hands
around to the back of his head. He felt his braid being loosened and then his hair tumbled down his back. She dragged
her fingers through it. Longer than mine, she whispered.

One by one, he pulled pins from her hair, and piece by piece
it fell in odd waves and curls, solid with perfumed lard. One
by one, the pins fell from his fingers to the floor and ticked
against the tile.

I think I will love you, she declared. She tried out the word:
Husband.

His fine hair fell around his face and hers and his heart

pounded in her sticky smell. With an exploring nose, he sniffed out the musk behind her ear and on the pulsing point of her neck.

Husband, husband, husband, she said, and let the word become familiar on her tongue—sung out in a trill to echo off the tiles.

He leaned over and blew out the lamp.

13

CORLISSA BEGINS WITH the ABC's.

The first time through, she takes Sai Fung's hand and guides her. Her pressure is gentle—anything more firm and she feels like she will sink through Sai Fung's flesh. Sai Fung's hand is cold despite a room so warm they don't even dare to open the curtains to the sun's glare. And in such proximity to Sai Fung, Corlissa feels dizzy, rocked on waves. A chill rides up her back. It must be the heat.

She settles back and watches them write. So Wai sits on her left, copying the words Corlissa has laid out already on a lined sheet: Hello, Thank You, Dear Friend, Sincerely. Like a child's primer, with the alphabet bordering the top. Their script is lovely—far more elegant than Corlissa's. Each stroke assertive, angling up or down with a flourish. Corlissa murmurs, Good, good. She says each letter, D, E, F.

D, E, F.

Good. Corlissa smiles. A tickle rises from her chest to her throat. She coughs. Excuse me.

Readjusts her sweaty grip on the pencil. She shows how to

swoop around for the curve in a G, the architectural strictness of H and I.

G, H, I.

G, H, I.

The humidity in the room grows. The curl is dropping from Corlissa's hair; she'll have to get it done. She pushes it off her neck with one hand and puts her other on So Wai's hand. Goose bumps stipple her skin when So Wai speaks in her sharp, deep voice.

J, K, L.

Corlissa's alphabet is nearly all lines and angles, while they manage to soften the letters, make them glide like arched bird bodies. So Wai's skin is just as chilly as Sai Fung's. It must be Corlissa who is withering in the heat.

You before studied this? she asks in awkward Chinese.

She doesn't miss the look that stretches past her between Sai Fung and So Wai. Sai Fung says, I used to work in a silk factory. Occasionally, a girl would come back from a city visit with sundries such as underwear and magazines. A tourist or missionary might pass an American magazine to her. I enjoyed looking at the letters, like little ants in busy formations.

Corlissa doubts her comprehension. She makes up words for those she doesn't understand, spackling the narrative into a type of poetry. Sai Fung continues, From what I understand, Sister So Wai has not studied English, but her calligraphy is wonderful. Right?

So Wai touches her beak nose and responds in monotone, You flatter me.

Corlissa turns to So Wai. Your husband when arrived here?

Six years ago, but I have heard nothing from him for a year. He worked on a ranch somewhere near here. A letter every few months, then nothing. The waiting was driving me mad.

Sai Fung—and you? You why came here? They answer her questions so readily, Corlissa pushes further.

The silk factory meant life in the dormitory, Sai Fung says. Many women were married—wives of down-on-their-luck farmers who needed to support their families. Others were single girls with few marriage prospects. I don't need a husband, but striking out was preferable to living in a room with nine other women until my hair grayed. She giggles.

Corlissa decides to cross the unasked. One never inquires how another arrived—on what sort of visa or lie. Those are the irrelevant fictions, but their spectacular arrival still gnaws at her.

How did you meet?

On the boat, Sai Fung declares.

An obvious answer. Corlissa blushes. She returns to the pages before her, readies for M, N, O, when So Wai says, There was an ocean. On one shore, it was gray. Black-bellied clouds, perpetual dusk. The people on the shore said the ocean was impassable. The horizon was the end of the world. She and I doubted them. Why else would there be a boat overturned and stuck in a sand drift? These were dead people who spent their days staring at the end of the world and lamenting. We cast off from the naysayers, floated for days across the sea. The end of the world was like a fleeing dragon's tail that we always approached, but never caught. Eventually, the sky lightened and land approached. Golden skies, sand like glittering glass. We're very glad to be here.

Corlissa frowns. The response is nonsensical to her. She understands each word, but put together, she loses their meaning. Literary allusions, metaphors, aphorisms and clichés she doesn't have access to. They're mocking her understanding, spinning a tale that would be absurd in any language. Drawn into their intimacy, then pushed out with a lie. She responds stiffly in English, Thank you for the story. Shall we get back to the lesson?

They're on her soil now. They might as well learn.

SHE STEPS OVER glass jewels, curls of poems, and softening fruit. Each has a tiny note tied to it with a greeting and a name. The men are indiscriminate about who their gifts go to. She'll scoop them up later. A shirtless man in coveralls naps on the lawn. He jerks his head up, sees it is only she and settles back to sleep. This has become a common occurrence since the women arrived. Ignored, Corlissa continues on.

CORLISSA NOTICES THE walls first. Despite the fancy, framed pictures of village scenes cut out of tissue and carried over from China, and the decorative shrimp made of plaited

palm leaf, fingerprints mark the walls from customers' children playing hide-and-seek among tables, or the proprietor's
own daughters trying to make some fun out of a long enclosed
day. The red-cloth lanterns are outlined in dust. All this is
especially clear to Corlissa in the afternoon light, which is
pure white pouring through the windows. She glances from
plate to plate on her way toward the back, hunger taking hold
from her tongue to her stomach.

Before the entrance to the kitchen, Yang's wife, Lucy, and
their niece sit at a table snapping beans. They talk as fast as
their fingers move. The ends litter the floor and the beans are
tossed back in the crate.

Hello, Corlissa! Lucy's switch into perfect English does not
break her momentum. Take a seat. She tells her niece to fetch
a drink and her uncle. Lucy is San Francisco born and she and
Corlissa have bonded over these common roots.

How's business? Corlissa joins in with the beans.

Lucy pushes hair off her face with the back of her hand.
So-so. One cook found work in Isleton, ranch cook, so Jack's
been back in the kitchen.

The news pleases Corlissa. And the help? she asks.

Not bad. A lazy bunch when they started, but they've got it
down now. Look at this—she waves her hand toward a piece of
paper tacked to the wall near the kitchen door. The days of the
week are written upon it in an awkward hand.

They're studying when they have a break. She smiles. How's
your daughter?

Her eyes stay on her work; an offhand question.

Corlissa bristles, then answers airily, Wonderful. She's been such a help with the women. We're teaching them English, though I'm not sure they'll need it to find work.

Our help has to be bilingual. Lots of Americans on the weekends. Another measured pause, then a nonchalant suggestion: The kids are going to pick seconds next month. Maybe Sofia would like to join. Something new, maybe interesting. Corlissa has heard of the summer ritual of letting kids loose on the remains of the pear harvest left in the orchards.

If not these children, then who has Sofia been running around with...? Corlissa blinks away the doubt and says she will let Sofia know.

So, how are they? I hear that Richard's wife has barely left their house. I don't know what he's hiding up there. Afraid she'll find out what kind of man her husband is. Corlissa marvels again at how quickly word travels in town. Lucy goes on: Strange. Why here? Show up with no connections, unable to trace back to anyone's village or sister's friend's cousin's husband or what-have-you.

They're fine. Helpful. Corlissa says it with the city dweller's lingering need to put on a public face. Jack comes out in a dirty apron over a sweat-marked shirt and black slacks. He is just lighting a cigarette. He shakes her hand.

Would you rather talk near the register?

He's always trying to keep things from me, his wife laughs. Jack pulls up a chair and smokes as he watches them with the beans.

How's Howar? His cigarette ashes fall onto the discarded bean ends.

Busy. Off to San Francisco a lot, working with a church there. The niece sets a soda in front of her. Corlissa thanks her and continues: He thinks, as I do, it might be very helpful for the women if they could maybe find some work. Not only for money, but to make some connections, get situated. With the side of her hand, she blades the condensation off the glass. She measures Jack's expression.

It's a great idea, Lucy says. She starts to sweep the rest of the beans back into the waxed cardboard.

Jack smashes his cigarette into a glass ashtray. He lights another. His fingernails are hard tortoise shells, work-scarred and ridged in white. He scratches his face with his pinky, carefully holding the cigarette away from his skin. He flicks more ash onto the floor. Corlissa sips her soda. Lucy makes a play of lining the beans up vertically in the box, a useless task to turn her face from the tension.

I don't know, Jack says. I already have too many without papers. I'm getting nervous. And two unmarried women? They'd have to live in our house so Lucy could keep an eye on them. He coughs smoke toward the floor.

No, So Wai is married, Corlissa protests. She doesn't understand the caginess, the reluctance.

If you could get papers—any kind—I'd consider. He leans back and lets his arms fall by his side. I just have too many people right now. I can't cut any hours.

But Corlissa knows the hours are long, that most work all day, in every capacity, just for the housing and the tips. Only economic diligence will allow them to eventually escape the arrangement. She'll resort to blackmail. Threaten to turn them all in if he doesn't comply. An anonymous note to the Sacramento sheriff. Say it in a calm, low voice, dripping with the reason of compliance. She can only purse her lips and nod.

You're sure, Jack? Lucy asks, looking at Corlissa.

Jack presses his cigarette into the tray, where it lies a discarded body among other ashed corpses. He flicks the clinging ash off his fingers, turns his head at the sound of a bell, and says in Chinese, Customer. I'm sorry, Corlissa. Then he stands up and greets with smiles and loud words the white couple standing nervously at the door.

14

SHE LAYS ORANGE peel at the foot of the stairs, and
in the morning the white pith crawls with snails. Richard
tosses the peel and it disappears beneath the awkward foundation of the house next door. She was going to eat them. The
kids still gather snails for their mothers to fry in garlic, but
Richard has lost his taste for them. He rolls his neck on his
shoulders in a cringing disgust. She might have fed them to
him. He might have eaten them, thinking they were wedges of
thick meat. He'll have to show her the market and that food
can be bought from orderly rows of stacked goods contained
in clean and fresh boxes and jars, sanitized and preserved. He
shudders again.

The keys to the Lucky Fortune hang on a discreet brass ring
that rests in his pocket. Twenty steps west and he is already
on Main. The town is busy—the morning rush of people to
work, stores opening, things forgotten the day before now
purchased. The clamor will fall off during midmorning, rise
up again for lunch, then slump until the late afternoon, when
the men come in from the ranches, buy up the beer in the cold

cases of the grocery stores and sit in the dropping sun, sighing off the day. Richard brushes past people on the narrow walkway, hello here, hello there, and arrives at the bolted doors of the Lucky Fortune. The first key fits into this lock. He slides back the wood bar, reveals access to the second lock—the one embedded in the door itself. Second key, turn, and he opens the door.

Complete darkness inside. No windows and even the skylight has been boarded up since the raid by the cops who came in blackface with more of their number dropping in from the top. He turns on the smoke-colored lights, then steps from table to table lighting the kerosene lamps as insurance to a blackout. That too a precaution from a robbery three years before: a man who backed up to the switch, scratched his back against the wall innocently, and turned off the lights so his partner could sweep the table and the register and disappear out the door with all the money by the time a hand could fumble to the switch again.

Water is set boiling, newspapers straightened. He looks up at the framed map of China and imagines Ming Wai's route—from their village settled just over the hill from the sea, through the water, off the map, ending somewhere near that wall groove. He turns the corner and unbolts the cashier's office with the third key. He makes sure there is enough money in the till, and that all is ready for the "One Thousand Character" classic lottery that is played twice a day. The housebound women send children out with their picks, but there are also two runners paid by the Lucky Fortune to go out collecting wagers. Ten characters for twenty-five cents. If all ten match those drawn, the winnings can be as high as a thousand dollars, guaranteeing a nice tip for the runner. The hope overcomes the risk.

The front ringer squawks. Richard leaves the office, locks the door behind him and looks through the peephole. The guard, Perry. Richard unbolts the door and lets him in. Perry nods hello. He sucks on a butterscotch candy; his cheeks flutter like a nursing calf's. Richard returns to the office; Perry will be left to check the peephole, let in customers, buzz the back if there is suspicion. With his straight-shouldered walk, he first goes to pour some tea before taking up his post at the front door.

Richard has been manager of the Lucky Fortune for four years. At first, he was ambitious. He politicked to become a partner so he could get the merchant status that would allow him to bring over Ming Wai. The competition was tight—everyone needed those papers. He'd bribed a little, argued some, then finally settled into his current position without complaint. The women were soft to him, sympathetic, leaned closer because he was safe. They treated him, a lonely husband, like an orphaned child. They stroked his hair, forgave his tantrums.

He sweeps out the office, dumps the dust and paper bits into the trash bin. The other two guards arrive, then the dealers. At ten, the men start trickling in; the flow rises until noon, when the tables are full, the refreshments on the back table gone, and Richard must refill the tea.

He is paid in a cut of the house. He soothes the customers, offers perks to remain competitive with the Ho Yoi Ling Sing next door. He supposes that each of the gambling places in Locke have a certain clientele. The Lucky Fortune has higher stakes, better snacks and faster dealers. Though most of the gamblers are ranch workers, it boasts a fair number of out-of-towners and weekend revelers from beyond the Delta. Richard's English skills have also drawn a certain percentage of whitemen. And then there is his friendship (yes, friendship now—no longer love, he thinks, surprised) with Madam See. A boy sent across the street like a call ahead. He provides the men; she provides the women.

Leaning on the counter, toothpick held between his teeth, Richard watches the noon hum and thrum. He reaches over and brushes some tobacco off the counter with his hand. Free Prince Albert tobacco for all the patrons. A man comes over to exchange buttons for cash. They'd replaced the chips and other paraphernalia with more innocuous items, like buttons and thimbles, after the raid. Lack of evidence meant one less thing they could be charged for. Richard watches over the exchange between the cashier and the customer. The toothpick has softened and splayed. He drops it into a spittoon behind the counter.

He believes in a grim watchfulness rather than open friendliness. He smiles occasionally, always listens in on the dirty jokes, but tries to maintain the distinction that marks him as a manager. Better than all that. Shirts pressed, pants creased, cuff links even. He has Poppy shave him and massage his face with her lotions. He thinks that hair kept a little longer than is the fashion shows the luxury to wash and brush it. He'd once heard one man say he was a dandy. He scoffed and threw the man out.

Richard leaves the cashier's office again, locking in the cashier behind him, and steps up the narrow stairs that turn once on a three-foot-wide landing. The ceiling is low, more like a rising tunnel to the top floor. He emerges into the slanted, low-roofed upstairs room. A twin bed with an iron frame for napping guards or the occasional night watchman. Dusty screens are built into the walls, shaded so that one can look down over the gambling floor beneath without being noticed. He keeps his dealers honest this way. In the attic heat, he rolls his sleeves, unbuttons the top of his shirt. He looks over the whole of the Lucky Fortune as if it is a toy world, manipulated by his godly hand.

He moves between the overlook room and the downstairs throughout the day. He moves among the customers, glancing over tables, saying hello, asking about a business venture, a wife or a mistress. He pours tea for some, rolls a cigarette for one. The afternoon cook fixes him some food that he eats upstairs; then he cleans his teeth with another toothpick, chewed on until long after lunch. In the alley next to the Lucky Fortune, he leans against the wall, feels nothing of the excitement flashing inside, and watches Manny Chow cheat people out of their winnings with a few thrown marbles. The day is falling off and the alley lights have come up.

At ten, he goes through the process in reverse: money in the safe, locked, cashier's office locked, burner turned off, kerosene lamps extinguished, lights off, door locked and bolted. Confucius believed ritual was the key to discipline. Here, his ritual is disrupted. He turns west, rather than east, and goes to Chloe, rather than home.

SOFIA COMES OUT the back door, a blanketed girl descending into fog. Chloe turns and leads. Bare feet against the damp sawdust-laid path between the gardens and through a tunnel of fennel that rises above their heads. To their right, just beyond the fog, pigs grunt outside the slaughterhouse. The coyotes, prone to a howl on bright-moon nights, are silent.

They go to the Hangman's Tree, a wild-haired oak with claw branches. A few years before, children pushing their way to the river had come upon feet, then looked up to see a man's dangling body. The place where the rope met the branch creaked with his weight. The men came and cut him down and the children, hand-whittled fishing poles still slung against shoulders, gasped as the body thudded onto the grass.

But that is a few years past and Chloe doesn't believe in ghosts, she whispers to Sofia. She breaks her way through the sedge. It saws against her trousers and folds under her heels. She nestles into a wide rising root. Sofia pushes in beside her.

Chloe removes a brown soda-water bottle from her jacket

and pries out the bit of broken cork that she has stuffed in its opening. The smell is instant.

I brought this for you.

Rice wine? Sofia asks.

Just a bit I siphoned out of a bottle.

You won't get in trouble?

No.

The glass is heavy and thick and the liquor inside faintly cloudy. Sofia puts her lips to the bottle and tips it slowly. At first touch of liquor to tongue, she rights the bottle.

It's so strong! Mrs. Chow makes this in her bathtub?

Chloe laughs. Not her bathtub, but yes, she made it. You have such a daydream of my life, don't you? She might have gotten mixed up. You know, she hides the stuff with her bathroom cleaners.

Sofia readjusts the blanket around her shoulders and tries the bottle again. Her face, under the canted light sifting through the oak branches, is dappled silver and dark curves. One brown eye brightly lit.

Mama acts as if she knows something, Sofia says.

How do you know? Embarrassment spills over Chloe's face like a knocked glass of red wine. Being an outcast is still a fresh wound.

Oh, she never says anything. It's looks, just looks. Sofia plays down the gossipy aspect of her revelation by running her fingers over the blanket piping and watching the piling brush down.

We don't have to meet.

She doesn't know. She thinks it's a boy.

Everybody knows. It's a small town. They just act as if they don't.

I don't care. Sofia's face turns pink from the liquor. Have some, Chloe.

Chloe refuses. She rests her head against the tree trunk and pulls at the grass.

Tell me what you do up there.

Chloe closes her eyes. Her fingers twist over and under blades of grass.

Tell me. Why doesn't Mama think you're worth saving?

The ground beneath rumbles. A vibration that grows and rocks and then is joined by the chuffing of an approaching train. A whistle sounds. Chloe puts her hands over her ears. Sofia takes another swig.

The branches shake; an acorn falls. The grindstone squeak of metal against the rails. The rising falling rising falling sound fades as the train heads south.

If you don't answer me, I'm going home.

Chloe tries to gauge what Sofia wants. What will satisfy her? Only grit. Sofia wants grit and dirtiness. Chloe can show her that. She undoes her shirt buttons and pulls her collar to the left, juts forth her shoulder. Despite the dark, Sofia can make out the bruise that sits beneath the ledge of Chloe's collarbone. You know what this is? Chloe asks.

Sofia recoils a little—Chloe sees the small pull backward, the reassessment of the situation made in the flutter of blinking lashes.

A hickey. Chloe drops her hand. The shirt stays open, revealing pale skin and a camisole strap. Richard Fong, she says.

Sofia settles back into the trunk, gathering her damp dark nightgown around her knees. I think I'm drunk.

Chloe splits strands of grass. Shredded slivers fall to the ground. It doesn't matter, it doesn't matter, does it?

Sofia puts her hand on Chloe's. Stop moving. Her hand slips from Chloe's waist to the small of her back. Her head on Chloe's shoulder. Rice wine odor flares from her nostrils. She burps and giggles.

Chloe stays very still.

Sofia unfolds her legs. The wine bottle falls over and drains with a glug glug. Her nose down Chloe's jaw, tracking a scent. Drugstore perfume splashed onto a finger and smudged along the side of a neck. It begins sweet and fades like rubbing alcohol. It's late, she whispers. Only the pulse in Chloe's neck against Sofia's mouth moves.

It's time to go. I've been gone too long.

Sofia jolts away, regathers her blanket, burns with liquor and embarrassment. Chloe sees her wake from the slow time of being tipsy, not quite sure what she's done or revealed.

15

Spring Morning Sun (1928)

YOU NOTICED HER and your stomach went weak the way it never had. She was just a whore, you told yourself, and you scanned her from the gleam of her rayon stockings to her over-rouged cheeks. She was just a whore, and maybe it was this that excited you. She was more exotic than anything else—a whitewhore in a Chinese town—the lowest of the low. She was silent and conspicuous, blond-haired, in the grocery store, her heels clicking down the wood floors. And nobody seemed to notice, but they moved aside at just the right moment, pressed closer to the shelves of oatmeal and cereal and boxed dried grits. She was the same height as you, maybe a bit taller, but she had breasts, and hips, and you measured yourself against her in a second-long look. You watched her go to the counter and try to smile at the grocer, so you stepped away from the magazines, closer to her.

She was buying a cola. She held out her palm, and the nickel that lay there was damp and warm, a talisman against the nonlooks and turned heads. All for a bottle of cola, already starting to sweat a few moments out of the fridge.

It was the first day of spring. Not by the calendar, but by the weather, and you were new to town, new to the valley. You were unused to mornings that started out warm and got warmer.

You followed her out—you didn't know why. Your mother would have whipped you if she knew and yet you kept walking, pushed through the doors and onto the sun-warmed storefront. She sat on the bench and there was a hiss when she tapped the bottle against the edge of the wood and the cap popped off. She was pretty, and you compared her to the only truly beautiful thing you had seen in your life—strips of burnt wallpaper floating across the bay and falling into the sea. She was pretty like singed paper on the wind.

But you didn't have these words—only a faint sense of the image and the feeling that arose. You couldn't even really think about your pulse, as you felt it in your chest and neck and wrists and thighs, or what your skin-flush in the spring morning sun meant, because this you had never even conceived of: that a girl could love a girl.

16

THE SOFT-PAD SOUND of skin on wood. A feral cat stink rises from under the buildings, where chicken wire has failed to keep the cats from nesting. Her mind is on sneaking, on a missed appointment, and on what has and has not happened. The tickle of Sofia's mouth on her neck like a phantom itch disturbs her. She peeks onto Main Street, switches her head back and forth. Empty. She scurries across and up to the side of the brothel. George naps on a stool just inside the door. He stutters out a greeting and pushes up his sleeves, exposing an epic tapestry of hunchbacked philosopher men with walking sticks and long wispy beards, fat-mouthed carp with scales outlined in green and filled in orange, gowned maidens making love to huge squid.

M-M-Mr. Fong is u-upstairs. His voice is soft, hesitant; it anticipates its own hiccuping sound. D-do you want me to c-come along?

Chloe shakes her head. She wipes each foot on the trouser leg of the opposite. She goes upstairs to the red room. Small earthquakes shudder her chest.

Richard sits in the chair facing the door. One booted foot propped on the other knee, he leans back in a pose of languor.

Ten-thirty, we said ten-thirty, right? he asks. He slowly unbuttons his right cuff and folds it back to look at his watch. Chloe shuts the door, but does not move from the doorway.

And here, it says eleven-thirty.

Chloe keeps her hand at the knob. She rubs her heel on top of her other foot. She glances down. There is still damp grass clinging to her toes.

Frolicking? he asks. Sit down. On the bed.

Such a strange word to use: frolicking. Chloe sits at the edge of the bed.

He leans forward and chucks her chin. He pushes some hair behind her ear. Leans back. I didn't see my wife for years. She might think it had something to do with you.

I'm sorry. Her meek words barely drift from her mouth. She braces a moment; the force of his palm knocks her jaw into her shoulder. The pain is surface, the stinging skin. She won't cry. Her heart pounds, but she won't cry.

It won't leave a mark, he says. It's because of me that you eat. That other men don't fuck you. He places his hand over the shape of it on Chloe's cheek.

Chloe is no longer there. She is at a hundred different points in her life. She is in the same body she had at thirteen, fourteen, fifteen, sixteen, with all the same feelings. She deserves this. She has been good, as good as she can be. What she thought she has paid back has returned: the wrath of her dead baby played out in the hand of a full-grown man. She doesn't think of Richard, or the reaching light, the streaks of red and gray stretching up and down the walls. She just feels familiar. She feels like home.

Who was it?

No one. I was out for a walk. I lost track of time.

Who were you out with? He walks back and forth with the pace of a smoking man.

She shouldn't shout. Indifference. She decides upon indifference. Lies back on the bed and looks for funny shapes in the texture of the wallpaper. A dancing goat, a little old man with sorrowful eyes. Richard holds a tight, thin roll of bills toward her. She ignores his hand and he sets it on the nightstand.

She unbuttons her shirt, flays it open. Unhooks her camisole, frees one arm from its strap, exposes a breast. She looks up at him and her fingers go to the button of her pants. His faith in his own good looks and charm leads him astray. He reaches out and touches the hickey. She wriggles her hips and slides her pants down.

Stop, he says. She follows his eyes to the waistband that girdles her thighs. I don't want you tonight. He picks up his money from the nightstand, unrolls and snaps out the bills. A moistened finger strums the top as he counts. Pull up your pants. It's one thing to be a whore; it's another thing to act like one.

Takes the hat off the peg behind the door. He leaves without a good-bye.

Chloe takes a small tin of ointment from the nightstand

drawer. She's been toyed with, threatened with affection and desire by both of them. She dips her finger in. The ointment is half gone. The petroleum dollop is cold on her fingers. She rubs it onto her cheek and the hot handprint turns to ice. Her cheek numbs. She replaces the lid and pushes the tin back into the drawer.

THE WALK FROM Chloe's to home. Richard presses one hand against the other and feels the strain all the way down to the tendons in his wrist. A faint tingling on his palm. He decides to go to the river.

He is walking past the packing shed when he hears a splash. Quiet, like a fish leaping for a fly. But then there's a whisper.

He eases his hands along the seam of the door, pushes gently to see if it will yield. It is locked, but there, around the corner, the platform edges over the water and he remembers that there is a ladder nailed to the side. He steps over quietly. A wind nips around the building and the river is veiled with mist. Splashing again; it comes from beneath him. He kneels, slowly, curls his hands over the edge, straightens onto his stomach, and looks over. He finds the bodies where they break the light on the water. They're only kids. Her hair is wet, slicked back, dripping onto the water. His hands are on her cheeks. She smiles, but his face is darkened and absent under her shadow.

Culled fruit and cores bob in the water around them.

Richard's disgusted that they would swim in such water, so late at night you can't see what's beneath, all for the sake of a tryst. He prefers the strictures of a set love affair. The couple moves into something more intimate and, despite his urge to watch and watch, he pushes himself up, brushes his hands together, and continues home.

Chloe's light is off already. Shame settles on him. Maybe he should apologize. But he feels this same guilt every time (never more than that first time, when she cried like she'd never been hit before) and he knows it will pass. Across from Wah Lee's boot place, he turns between the fish market and his house. His front door is recognizable by the odor of fish guts, dumped into a pit by the market, to be burned twice a week. The knotholes are enough to release the scent. On the days between burnings, cats yowl over the boards. Richard stamps his feet at the cats and goes inside.

Ming Wai has fallen asleep on the sofa. There is something sunken about her; she appears the color of old chicken skin. Richard steps forward to rouse her, pauses. She smells unclean, as if the baths he insists she takes, the perfumes he insists she wears, cannot scrub the sea from her.

He is intoxicated by women. He likes the folds where their secret smells lie, the pungent odors specific to them. Wispy hair and small ears and coquettish looks. He likes the coyness, the shyness that hints at something ravenous below the surface. The jut of a hip, the places where weight settles on the thighs. He wants it all. But Ming Wai seems too much.

Ming Wai wants touching. She trails him around the house, makes careful quiet note of every blink and swipe. The house, which once smelled like him—a smell absent in its familiarity, but to a stranger: cedar, aftershave, and sweat—now relents to her. Her breath, her gas, her sweat. With every breath, he is reminded she is here.

He leaves her asleep on the couch and goes to the bathroom instead. Slips off shoes, peels away damp socks, undresses. Steps into the bathtub. There it is again. The white ring around the edge of the empty tub. Richard crouches, bare feet against cold porcelain, and rubs his fingers against the ring, and the residue that comes up reminds him of—what's the word?—scouring powder. The kind that comes in a cardboard cylinder with a sieved metal top. The words come to him in English. Scouring powder. But it doesn't have the chemical smell. It's natural, oceanlike. It's the smell of Ming Wai's barely dented pillow in the morning, the smooth sheet where her body has lain. This is what comes off her body when she bathes? Not the scummy ring his own body leaves—gray, hair-flecked—but ice-white, softly grained like salt. He licks his fingertips and it tastes like his wife.

It tastes like his wife. He can actually create this phrase. A sense detail not out of a long-term memory, but actual salt on his fingers. His wife: He is part of a pair, linked decidedly to a single woman. Poppy and Chloe are suddenly transitory figures. He dips his finger into the drain and removes a hoop of tangled hair. It has snagged on what lies hidden, deeper in the curves of the pipe, and brings up with it wet lint and sloughed body dirt. This is her hair, washed from her scalp. It hangs on his finger.

He drops the hair onto the floor. He plugs the drain. He turns the faucets, mixing the hot and cold that flow from each. The water fills in the spaces between his toes, covers his feet, rises up his ankles, then his calves. He settles into it. He swirls the water where it meets, so that waves of cool and hot will not sweep past his skin. Steam begins to rise. The water touches the salt ring and he turns off the faucets. The water circles his neck. His knees bend into the air. The heat soaks into him like a fever coming through his arms and legs and chest. He coughs. Fever coming into his lungs through steam so thick it wets the inside of his mouth.

He coughs again. Water splashes onto the floor. He tries to clear his throat, dislodge what clings and renders his breath ragged. He thinks of sickness as he's known it: his father, his mother, a baby brother. There was the flu epidemic in 1919, and in one war after another, the sickness that spread out of the corpses that blocked the rivers. And then, in the stories: the obedient daughter who slices at her flesh for soup for a deathbed mother; a man who loses his life essence out of love for a ghost-woman. He coughs again.

With his toe, he pulls on the chain that holds the stopper. There is a gurgle, then a suck as the water drains.

17

The Pigskin Suitcase (1924)

UNDER THE BED was your suitcase. Made of battered paperboard covered in pig leather, it had lain under every bed you had slept in since your arrival in America. The clasps still opened with ease, you found, and the painted brass had barely flaked. Inside: an immigration visa of unadorned and buttoned-up black ink and, marked in a stranger's scrawl, your name (Fong Man Gum), the date (April 28, 1918), the port of entry (Angel Island), and the name of the vessel (the *Olympia*); a plain gray stone that did not even gain a shine in water, picked up from the enclosed yard of the Angel Island barracks; a folded cutout of red paper that, unfolded, was the Double Happiness character, still scented with the idea of fireworks at a wedding banquet; a sepia-tinted photo, splitting from its paper back, of your family; a square of crisply folded newspaper, the whole article unreadable in folded form, so that the exposed sides revealed only these lines of the Immigration Act:

A consular officer upon the application of any immigrant (as defined in section 3) may (under the conditions hereinafter prescribed and subject to the limitations prescribed in this Act or regulations made thereunder as to the number of immigration visas which may be issued by such officer) issue to such immigrant an immigrant visa which shall consist of one copy of the application provided for in section 7, visaed by such consular officer. Such visa shall specify (1) the nationality of term "alien" includes any individual not a native-born or naturalized citizen of the United States, but this definition shall not be held to include Indians of the United States not taxed, nor citizens of the islands under the jurisdiction of the United States; (c) The term "ineligible to citizenship," when used in reference to any individual, includes an individual who is debarred from becoming a citizen of the United States under section 2169 of the Revised Statutes, or under section 14 of the act entitled "An Act to execute certain treaty stipulations relating to Chinese," approved May 6, 1882.

and a long braid of black hair that once hung down your back out of loyalty to the emperor and was shorn in 1911.

18

THE BARBER'S HAND is shaking. He is overworked, and the pain stretches from wrist to elbow. His assistant, lovesick, has quit, and the scraggly-haired men crowd the chair, lean against the window ledges, and spill out the door. They must be trimmed by churchtime Sunday. There are fights in the street and in the fields over empty boasting and triumphant claims. This one has stolen a kiss from the younger woman, he says; another saw one changing clothes through the blue church windows. The barber works his razor carefully over a man's jaw, wipes the blade on a rag, catches himself in the mirror. His age shows in his neck, loose and mottled. His hair is mussed and ragged too, but who cuts the barber's hair? When will it be his chance to court these women? He was in love with a girl in his hometown. He hardly knew her, and over twenty years have passed, but he holds on to the love so he can say he has someone too. The blade scrapes along hard stubble and lather. Would it sound the same dragged down a woman's leg? He wipes it down again and tosses it into the basin. No more. The man in the chair is half shaved, waiting for the next pull of metal against his skin, but the barber is gone.

19

HOWAR TAKES CORLISSA by surprise. She goes to him at his desk in the corner of the living room, looks with displeasure at the mess fanning across it—the loose paper, pens, roll of stamps unfurling—and asks if he is ready to go.

He asks where they are going and when she reminds him that it is the Fourth of July, that they have never missed the fireworks, he caps his pen and gives a long look at his desk. He asks if it is obvious that he can't go. She'll have to drive by herself and Corlissa gives a huffing sigh because Howar knows that she fears driving the road at night. Everything is pitch-black, and the only indication of the river, the only warning to keep on the levee, is the moon shining off the water. The one time she drove the levee road at night, she crept slowly, shuddering at every bump.

You know I can't drive that road at night, she says. She tries to see what is written across all those papers, but can catch only a word or two; nothing illicit revealed. Suddenly Howar rises from his chair; it swivels and rolls backward; he presses himself against her. She's backed to the wall. She turns her face away and whispers, What are you doing? He has his mouth to her ear, his fingers in her hair. She's angry, but she giggles, Howar, stop it! He kisses her lobe. She tries to wiggle away. She looks out the window at the two women sitting beneath a tree, digging away at a fruit. A pomegranate. Their mouths and fingertips are red.

They might see us, she whispers. But outside it is much brighter than the shadowed living room and all they will see in the window is themselves. She pushes against his hips with her palms and says, I don't know what's the matter with you.

Your hair smells different, he says. She's self-conscious, blushes, says it's the permanent. He nods, reaches hands back to feel for the chair, and sits down. He rocks in his chair and repeats, I can't go.

She's still light-headed from his sudden closeness, then distance. She nods her head, yes, yes, yes, but the questions are waiting—not at the tip of her tongue, but farther back, where there is only the wonder but not the language. The whole world is different. For days now, she has given second glances to everyone. Her daughter, her husband, the people in town. She feels like her grandmother, who once reached the point when the world was far too different than what she'd known. She couldn't negotiate the new rules, etiquette, language, politics. After spewing curses and spittle at Corlissa as explanation, it had been as simple as willing herself to stop breathing. Howar has turned back to his desk, but Corlissa still leans to the wall, mesmerized. The women outside the window cast the pomegranate rind to the grass. They are always there, in the corner of her eye, just past the window, just through a doorway. Sparks are lighting in her mind, feeling like the jolts of static electricity she gets when touching a doorknob. Howar is as unhappy as she is. His eruption of passion was antagonistic, the kiss given when one really wants to bite. Small epiphanies are erupting that she will forget as soon as she is back in the banality of day-to-day. She welcomes all the knowledge, still leaning against the wall, breathing, thinking, ignored by her husband, for once enjoying life, until her mind darkens again and she goes to pack for the fireworks.

20

THE THEATER IS cool.

Chloe wants to be in the dark where the heavy red drapes pull back to reveal a screen, and the springs press up through the red plush seats. Every shift elicits a squeak. The talkies have made their way to Sacramento, but the Walnut Grove theater hasn't yet been renovated for sound. Chloe comes to sink into her chair and watch the flicker of black and white across the screen. She's not sure who the characters are, what they are doing, if they're in love. She can't get lost in the fiction of it.

Sofia has gone to Sacramento for the night with her family and the boat-women. And when Chloe heard the shuffling of Madam See in her closet and the heaviness of a bottle removed, she knew that she was free for the night. Some of the other girls have gone out with their boyfriends, and one is visiting home. They have all left to George the task of grabbing at Madam See's wrists when the numbness of the alcohol fades, when she starts to cry out before her head tips into sleep. No one has stayed to mop the floor of her vomit, or receive the lash of her drunken tongue.

Chloe brings her feet up to rest on the back of the chair in front of her. She leans her head back and the cold metal of the chair's frame presses into the bend of her neck. Home for her is not so far away. San Francisco too is not so far away, and she knows where Alfred stays. He left her, in New York and without heat, for a brass-and-white apartment in San Francisco and a woman named Dixie. Both of them, stinking of money. They were living—and she had too!—the promised moneyed life that the people in Locke only dreamed of. Maybe couldn't even dream of.

She knows how words move down the streets and up and down the alleys until the town is suffused with gossip, but she wonders how they travel along the river. Do they dip into every waterway, every slough and creek and island? Have they flowed so far that her mother knows that Chloe is so close, just a few towns over, and living in a brothel built for Chinese men?

A shaft of light breaks down the center aisle as the door in the back opens. Two whispering boys clop down the aisle and take seats a few rows ahead, on the other side of the theater. When the glare of the sudden light-blindness fades and Chloe's eyes have readjusted to the dark, she glances at the latecomers. They are teenagers, gangly, but still to grow. She wonders what brings them into a theater on the Fourth of July when everyone else is out having a family picnic and waiting for the fireworks to start. There is the rustle of waxed paper removed from a bundle of candy. More whispers, which resonate in the nearly empty theater. A couple turns toward them and the man says, How 'bout you keep it down? The boys laugh.

The hair feathering the nape of one boy's neck is familiar. So are the shape of his head and the slouch of his shoulders. Even in light that rises and falls, she recognizes the gold-touched hair and the curve of his ears. He was ten when she left, at school on the afternoon that she hefted her bag and set out to hitch for a ride on the highway. He'd be twelve now, nearly thirteen?

She dares herself to whisper his name, David, and loses the sound in the crackle of the paper and the shudder of the film feeding through the projector. The phonograph plays low and sticks into a groove. The melody repeats.

She puts her feet on the floor and sits up straight. She leans forward and utters his name like a length of smoke.

David.

David.

David, David, David.

He pauses and looks at his friend. He says something, his friend says something, and both turn back. She quickly looks at the screen. When she dares to glance again, they are watching the movie.

Her heart pounds. What message will she send back to her mother? What will she tell, and what won't she tell? What will she tell for his ears only, some secret he can hold as a bond between the two of them? The figures on the screen are completely lost to her.

The screen shakes a little when the thundering outside begins. The music is consumed by each crack of the fireworks. The man takes his arm off his girlfriend's shoulders and turns back, squinting up toward the projector. Chloe feels the pound in the pulse of her neck. The boys look around in gleeful surprise. Her brother removes a peppermint stick from his mouth and says something to the other boy. They stand up.

They are leaving; each beat and burst takes them one step closer to the door. They pause before Chloe.

Hey, don't you want to see the fireworks? David says with a grin.

Two years older than he was, with shadows of the adult face he will have. His face looks darker, his jaw sharper.

She smiles. I want to see the rest of the movie.

The man calls out, You aren't the only ones in here! Chloe glances at him and smiles back at David.

David's friend is walking again toward the door. David starts to shake his head, as if to say, Crazy girl, giving up fireworks for romance in black and white. But he stops and squints at her. They look at each other, then his glance passes through—the moment of recognition slides by.

Suit yourself, he says. He resumes sucking on the candy and follows after his friend.

Chloe does not turn to watch them leave. She wants the blood to subside, the geyser-flood from heart to face, the geyser-rush in her ears and the tingle in her fingers. Home seems closer. Her past is real again. The blood from her birth has drained through her mother's bedsheets into this same soil. Whatever she was looking for among high-rises and neon lights was not home.

The fireworks reach a frenzy—it must be the finale. The picture jumps with the layered explosions. Then the whine of the phonograph fills the theater once again and spins out the last of its song. The screen flickers to black.

21

The Split Water Blues (1926)

THERE HE WAS, beneath Chloe's window, whispering as loud as a shout.

Chloe! Chloe!

Chloe scrambled over to the window.

Oh, Jesus, Chloe, he said in a high whisper. Come out and walk with me?

Chloe glanced back at her brother sleeping and her mother dead gone in the corner of the room. Her father, thank goodness, was still on his shift and the dog stayed curled up—so lazy it wouldn't stir if a rat nibbled on its tail.

All right, she said. Shut up, I'll be out.

She grabbed her daddy's big plaid shirt, the red woolly one that she wore like a jacket because these nights got chilly with the Delta breeze.

Outside, Barrett stomped his feet in the cold.

Sorry to bother you, Chloe. I just, you know, wanted to talk to you.

She giggled. He really was drunk; it was all over him in the iron smell of his sweat.

Come on.

They made an arc, clearing the houses and the small speak-easy still erupting with sound.

You want to go back there? he asked. He nodded toward the tule reeds that formed a barrier to the water. A small trail led to the edge. It's dark, he said, but look. There's a half-moon.

I'd rather walk around here.

Yeah, yeah. I don't want to make you uncomfortable. I just, you know, wanted to talk. Every time he made this admission he tugged at a tuft of his strawberry hair.

If you're not careful, Chloe giggled, you'll pull it out.

What? Oh, yeah. I just, you know... Well, you know.

They walked silently, the tapping of their feet on the dirt louder than anything except the flap of bat wings.

They carry rabies, Barrett said. So, you think you want to stay here when you get older? I mean, me, I got all these things I want to do.

They found themselves in the middle of someone's tomato patch. A few ripe ones had fallen onto the dirt and split, sweet with rot.

Barrett continued to ask questions and answer them with his own hopes and thoughts, ending each with—I'm babbling. I don't know what I want to say. I just wanted to see you, Chloe.

Yeah, Chloe said, because she was only fifteen and didn't know yet what to say to men who cried for you from the depths of their drunkenness.

The chill seeped through her dad's jacket. I'd better get back before my daddy gets home.

Sure, sure. It's cold and I'm babbling. Well, good night.

Good night, Barrett.

Two days later he was cool to her. She figured it must have been because he remembered coming to her window stinking of whiskey in a jar and whispering for her to come out. She smiled at him to let him know she didn't care. She said his name at the end of hello, so he wouldn't feel embarrassed.

That night he was at her window again. Again she slipped out in her daddy's coat.

HE TOOK HER on the path through the wild licorice to a clearing where a flame-scarred brick foundation remained. A home in ruins. Blistered red paint still visible on the water pump. Some falling-over pieces of wood. Set off at the far edge of the clearing stood an outhouse, perfectly intact. Chloe sat on what was left of one of the house's walls.

Don't sit on that, Barrett said. He laid his own coat down and when she sat on it, he knelt before her and said, I drank only a little bit tonight, Chloe. I didn't want to come to you stinking.

He took a hand-rolled cigarette from his pocket and struck a match on the brick. The tobacco was sweet and he blew a ring with the first puff. Chloe stuck her finger through it so the ring broke into squiggly white lines in the night and she couldn't distinguish her own cold breath from his smoky breath.

You know that story where the women sing and make the Greeks smash their boats on the rocks? he asked.

No.

Well, you're beautiful like them. In school, the teacher said they had a voice to beat all—prettier than Helen of Troy's face. They made men smash themselves on rocks. I'd go to ruin for you.

But it was Chloe who tempted ruin, pressed up against the outhouse wall. His skinny hips wriggled out of his pants, the buckle pressing into Chloe's thigh.

THE STEPPING OUT was easier than she imagined. During the morning bustle, no one noticed. She simply walked onto the county road and hitched a ride to San Francisco. She was done with Barrett and mean-eyed gossip and the way her hometown roped her up so tight in her family history that she could hardly breathe.

From San Francisco, coach to Chicago on the Starlight Special. It was a twenty-nine-hour trip. One step out of the depot into the Chicago spring wind and Chloe knew she hadn't gone far enough. She bought another ticket—this one all the way to New York City.

NEW YORK.

New York awed her; New York disappointed her. The buildings were tall, but not tall enough. She tried to look up at the gray—gray roads, gray buildings, and gray people—while keeping pace with the foot traffic. She had no one to go to, so she wandered. The wind cut through her coat. This was not spring as she knew it—a girl brought up on Central Valley sunshine, whose hair already bore the sun-kissed streakiness of summer. A few blocks over she found a small café with a dulled sign reading Good Food and a poster advertising breakfast.

A brisk waiter with a flamboyant mustache seated her singly in a booth. He was impatient with her slow perusal of the menu, but how could she concentrate with the flurry of foreign tongues around her? She finally ordered eggs, bacon, rye toast, and orange juice. The waiter was just as brisk about her food.

She wanted to float in her sleepiness. She sipped her juice and looked around. An old woman was seated at the booth next to hers. She wore old-fashioned pointed-toe lace-ups and a hat with a tattered black veil. The waiter stood patiently as she reiterated her order: Toast, wheat toast, not too dry. And a biscuit with some butter. Did you hear me ask for toast? Wheat toast? And you have biscuits? I'd like just one, with my coffee.

The exchange bore the rhythm of routine. The woman clasped her hands before her, patiently waiting. A diamond sparkled in the morning sun. She turned her head and caught Chloe's eye with the look of a woman who has just happened upon a presence in her own living room. Chloe looked away.

Chloe dawdled over breakfast, reluctant to be thrust back into nameless wandering.

. . .

SHE RODE THE subway uptown. The rocking undercarriage lulled her toward sleep. The people were silent, eyes to themselves. A Chinaman entered the car through the rumbling space of the open door. He sold random things: mini manicure sets with tiny scissors and a tiny file; lollipops; tiny dolls that danced on strings; candied crabapples. He yelled these things out with a voice that Chloe strained to unravel. People stared; no one bought. He passed into the next car.

She disembarked at a random stop. To the west she saw a river. She walked down to stare at the golden brilliance wending its way through the hustle.

You should see it at sunset. A voice broke through Chloe's four-day aloneness. It belonged to a dapper man in a hat.

It's beautiful now, Chloe said, finding her voice and afraid it would crack from disuse.

He eyed her carpetbag and said, Far from home? Or leaving town?

I'm from California.

Far from home, then, he said.

Yes, far from home. Looking at him more closely, Chloe saw that he was handsome, young. Green eyes, black lashes, black hair. Italian? Or something she couldn't place, some ambiguous mix or race. The world contained in a city, in a face.

I'm Alfred.

Chloe Howell.

Then Alfred made a move, a move that made Chloe fall down inside. He took off his hat and said how pleased he was to meet her. He took off his hat, held its felt top in his palm, against his chest.

Chloe could only look at him, then squint back at the river.

Are you visiting family?

No, it's just me.

Friends?

No.

New York can be tough on a girl alone. He corrected himself: A woman alone. I was born and raised here, I can maneuver its streets a bit better. But you, California Girl....Do you even have a hotel? He eyed her bag again, the unraveling seams and chipped clasp. No, you don't. Let me buy you a cup of coffee.

I've had coffee, Chloe said. It jumbles up my stomach. I think, I think, I should go look for a place to stay.

An egg cream? A soda? Maybe a drink will calm you down.

It was real concern Chloe saw when she turned to him again. And he smelled so good, like fresh shaving cream lathered on a brush. He was so clean, from the milky shine of his shoes to the strict white lines of his collar.

THEY RODE THE subway to his flat in the Bronx.

He lived on the third floor where everything was new and white. Modern, like Chloe had never imagined. Furniture that curved rather than bent, a huge bay window, waxed tile floors that tinkled against Chloe's heels.

Alfred asked what she would like to drink. Chloe walked over from the window. Behind the bar, a mirror reflected back the neatly lined bottles of every height and shape, the contents varying in color. Gin, vodka, absinthe, brandy, rum, red wine. Alfred held out a thick crystal tumbler full of ice. Anything you want.

My god, Chloe said. She brought her hands to her face and cried.

ALFRED MADE HER. The first thing they had to do, he said, was get rid of her country look. He took her shopping down sidewalks swept clean, into shops with wood and brass interiors where the shopgirls called her ma'am and measured her with straight pins in their mouths. Skirts, blouses, dresses, even tailored pants. Sleek gowns for the evening, and over these, a fur-trimmed coat.

He took her to music clubs and dinner clubs with red-draped tables. Sometimes it was the two of them, sometimes his friends came along with their own women—women who laughed loud with big teeth and drank hard.

New York laughed in its wealth. It was 1926.

THEY BECAME REGULARS at the Scat Cat! Club in Harlem, mostly for a singer named Ruby Moore. Chloe thought of

Ruby as a swan because of her long neck. A birthmark, ruby-colored and shaped like a chrysanthemum, lay dead center on her throat. When Ruby tipped her head back in song, the chrysanthemum pulsed and fluttered its dozens of petals in the tide.

Chloe's favorite song—the one that would not leave her mind (even years later, engaged in chores at Madam See's)—was the "Split Water Blues":

> God dried up the Jordan
> He split the Red Sea
> but He can't
> (nuh-uh, He can't)
> bring back my man to me.

Chloe, pleased that she understood the references, spent the length of the song enraptured and wondering who was the man that drove such a song. She looked over at Alfred, feeling bluesy and sad for a lost moment in the melody.

Chloe was in love with Ruby Moore. Not in-love-in-love, she'd laugh if asked. In love the way a woman loves a woman. In love with precisely the womanliness of Ruby—the breasts that grew as Chloe's didn't, the hips that stretched the dress fabric until it shone. When she was silent during the song, Alfred said to his friends, Look at my little moll! She's head over heels for that bitch. If Chloe was silent, they found her intelligent and beautiful, so she replied with only a glance.

Ruby sent her secret messages. Only a woman knows what a woman knows, she sang, and Alfred nudged Chloe and laughed.

THE HUMID HEAT of a summer. In a roof garden with drinks and hors d'oeuvres. Listening quietly to conversations between women who sounded as if they had been born into wealth.

No, Alfred told her in bed, they're country like you. They couldn't tell a salad fork from a soup spoon.

So Chloe fell deeper into imagining Ruby's life. She followed her home from the club, to what she imagined was a fantastic home in Manhattan. Baroque, with gilded moldings. Ruby, with her harem of lovers.

Chloe fell out of love with Alfred—the way he sat around in his undershirt in the heat, talking angrily on the telephone; the way he smoked in front of the window so that it curled back into the room; the gun that traveled with him through the apartment, left on the dining table, on the vanity, on the nightstand.

SHE AWOKE TO hot metal pressed to her cheek. It was hot like it had been nestled against his side for the night.

You know I love you, Chloe, he said. The gun hard on her bone.

He scooted on top of her and squeezed her face, holding the gun with his right hand.

Don't you love the danger of me? Me, Chloe. She closed her eyes and prayed as he fucked her with the gun against her cheek.

Afterward, she lay still, waiting for morning, but fell asleep. When she awoke, she found a note on the table.

Sorry about last night. Off to San Fran. Alfred.

She stayed on, waiting for the cash he'd left to run out. She went to the Scat Cat! and wondered if her man would come back to her. She stayed through the snow, until people came to collect the furniture.

You can't! she said. She scurried back and forth following the men, and stood beside them as they lifted and left. That's our furniture! Alfred will be so upset! Please!

They called her Lady like they didn't care. They eyed her fat belly protruding through her robe. They left her with dishes, silverware, and thick crystal tumblers empty of ice. She slept on the dusty tile, a towel rolled under the small of her back.

At the end of March, she locked up the place, left the key in the mailbox, and took the train to San Francisco.

West, again.

ALFRED STOOD AT the window, lit by luminous fog. He had his back to the room. Sitting on the couch—a woman Alfred had introduced as Dixie. She wore nothing more than a slip, and she smoked a pipe full of sweet Indian tobacco.

No one spoke. Everyone waited for Alfred.

The apartment was even lovelier than the one in New York, with a view of cypress trees and the gray, foamy Pacific.

He hadn't even asked Dixie to leave the room. He knew what Chloe wanted and she waited for his answer. Would he go back with her? Would he let her stay?

The lights of the homes around them popped up gold, one by one, in the fog. The three sat in the darkening room. Silently, a maid slid in and pressed a switch. The lights came up sparkling in an electric chandelier.

They hadn't even offered Chloe a drink.

Alfred was stilted and silent. His discomfort surprised Chloe, because when they had, through some perversity of coincidence, passed on Market Street, he had given her his address.

Finally he turned from the window: Dixie, what's that place? That place for... He looked at Chloe's stomach without meeting her eyes.

Dixie leaned her pockmarked face forward to tap the tobacco into an ashtray. Her breasts swung beneath her slip: The Florence Crittenton Home?

Alfred walked to the table and wrote the name on a card. You can read, can't you? he asked Chloe.

She bit her lip against the comment. Florence Crittenton, she repeated.

Alfred flipped money out of his billfold and handed Chloe one hundred dollars. This ought to take care of everything. But this is it. You're a big girl now, Chloe. Back and forth across this country two times, all by yourself. Don't look for me again, all right?

You loved me? Chloe wished to make it a statement, but couldn't prevent the lilt at the end.

He finally met her eyes. His green eyes, those emerald eyes that glowed in twilight and glimmered under electric lights in a San Francisco apartment. There was the waiting of Chloe and Dixie for his answer.

You loved me? he asked.

Chloe paused. Had she? Who had she loved, ever? She busied herself putting the money into her handbag.

I'm ready to go, she said without looking up at him. She allowed him to show her to the door. As she crossed the threshold into the hall, a response came to her. She tilted her head toward him and said (if ever there was a moment when she needed strength, when she needed bravery)—

I loved the danger of you.

but He can't

There was a single heartbeat before he said, Good-bye, Chloe.

(nuh-uh, He can't)

'Bye, Alfred.
He shut the door while she still waited for the elevator.

bring back my man to me.

22

RICHARD DOES NOT know why he has so much fear when she kneels down in front of him. She brings her hand like a blade between his knees and opens his legs. She slides her hands from his knees to his thighs. He wants to stop her; this is what he means when he puts his hand on her head. Neither of them speaks, and she leans forward to unbutton his pants. When he squeezes her hair in his hand, tangles it in his fist, he means, Stop. He can't say it.

She licks him and sucks on him and he feels like he's getting weaker. The protests still roil inside him, but he can only open his mouth and breathe. He leans back onto the bed.

This is what they warn in the stories—women can steal your strength, your essence. Richard has always laughed, interpreting the idea of essence as a literal thing, but with his mouth going weak, his lungs going empty, essence feels more nebulous. He is unsure what it is, but is sure he is losing it.

She rises from the floor. She hitches up her dress and crawls onto him. His hands on her back, slipping under the shirt and to the skin—this means stop. His fingers pressing so hard he feels bone, this means stop. His heart-pound is fear, not pleasure, he tells himself.

Please look at me, she says. He opens his eyes and looks at her. The pallor of her face seems to be fading, even as they move. Her face takes on a color, a luminosity that it had lacked when she first came two weeks ago. She watches him carefully. Her eyes move from his eyes to his forehead, to his nose, to his mouth. She kisses him. His heart slows. The pump, as steady and measured as the ticking of a clock, fills his ears. So slow, he feels the blood fill one chamber and push out of another. He feels the muscles contract in their choreographed dance and the blood leave his chest.

His hands slide off her back and fall to the bed. She puts her hands on both sides of his face and holds him, kisses him. Her mouth is salty. He thinks of the shore, rather than the water. Blood fills one chamber. It pumps out of the other. He's too weak now to kiss. His mouth goes still and she moves her lips insistently over his. She covers his mouth with hers and he hiccups for breath. He closes his eyes and waits for the waves.

When it is over, when he opens his eyes again, she is above him, smiling. She seems to glow—her cheeks are flushed, her eyes shine like wet ink.

She drops her face into his neck and murmurs, You're so pale.

Richard feels his heartbeat gain strength and start to quicken. He touches his forehead; it feels gray and cool. I feel like you've drained my life away.

She giggles, and her laugh is a hot vibration against his cold neck.

ON THE UPPER level of the Yuen Chong, they flip through dresses. Scarlet, flame-orange, purple like blood flowing under skin. Ming Wai pulls a low-waisted, ice-blue silk dress off the rack.

Siu Dai's wife had a dress this color, she says.

Pretty, Richard says. He nods at a woman, the Chinatown-born wife of one of the restaurant owners. She scurries past, distracts herself with men's slacks. The store owner's daughter wipes down a glass case. The gloves and handkerchiefs inside it splay in multicolored rainbows.

I wish you could see their children, Ming Wai continues as she looks down at the silk rippling off the hanger. Ga Jeun is a funny little piglet, always playing pranks, but a real mama's boy.

The fan ticks lazily, pink string fluttering off the blades to scare the flies.

And Mui Mui is a mean little witch. The boys go crazy over her. Morning glares through the window, hazing the air. Richard doesn't want to discuss children with her. Try it on, he says.

Ming Wai glances at him with surprise, looks at the uninterested salesgirl, then slips behind a slatted folding screen. You should see your father's house. Siu Dai bought an electric refrigerator. I really don't know why you left. It's a more comfortable life there. An unseen hand flings over the old dress from Corlissa Lee. She emerges like a shimmer of water. She turns in the three-way mirror.

Lovely, says the girl from the counter.

Ming Wai holds up her hair, looks at the line from armpit to hip, the flatness over her belly. She's as beautiful as an advertisement, selling face lotion or bug spray. Richard can see her painted across bricks on the side of a city building, the blue dress like glass windows reflecting the sky.

She's got the perfect flapper figure, the girl says.

Richard nods.

Wear it home, he urges. He's feeling generous. Billfold out, fingers across the bills. Clang of the register, pop of the drawer. The shush shush of rustling silk, his hand on her back.

23

SURPRISING TO POPPY'S ears, the morning world is silent. She expects to hear liveliness below—women laughing, men talking, even George lumbering about, but there is not even the settling of walls.

The stink of her own vomit on her blankets and nightdress has awoken her. Clear wet stains smeared across cloth that smells of gin. The first drink always makes her cringe, but she feels better and better until she does not know how much, how long. The bottle stands half full on the nightstand, delicately placed. Despite the way her muscles feel—soaked with liquor—she knows that if the bottle is upright, the night has not been too bad.

The silence bothers her. The girls must be huddled together in their attic room, giggling over her, anticipating her wake-up. Or perhaps they are whispering while George nods on. Poppy sits up and steps out of bed.

All her perceptions are askew—the floor is much too far, the door is too wide, and though she holds her head straight, she feels as if she walks leaning to the side. She pulls her damp nightgown over her head and replaces it with an old housedress. She pours a little water into the basin on her vanity and cleans her face with it, scrubs at her mouth, runs her wet finger along her teeth. Now there is sound: her hands sloshing water in the porcelain bowl, the brush of her hands against her face. Here is the sound of her bare feet across the floor, the way the wood eases to each step, and the sound of the door swinging on its hinges. In the hall, she is more careful with sound. She wants to launch upon the girls in the midst of their disrespect. She wants to hear them laughing at her.

She takes each step with consideration. If she hurries, the stairs will creak. The stairway is dark, walls on both sides, lit by only the weak sun in the crack under the attic door and the light on the bottom steps that comes from the house. She pauses at the door. She holds her breath. All the heat from the house has welled up at this uppermost point and swells before the door. Behind it, the attic is quiet.

She opens the door and steps into the musty gray room. She hunches to avoid the sloped ceiling and walks between the two rows of beds to the small diamond window. The roof peaks a little here and she rises on her tiptoes to peer out. The window is kept clean, spit-wiped. She looks down onto the river road, at the Southern Pacific warehouse on the other side, and at the river that runs under and around the warehouse. People bustle about, but she does not recognize any of them.

The silence means she is alone. She lies down on one of the beds and looks at the ceiling. There is little between a sleeping body and the roof except heat. She is hot and hung over and alone. She tries to pretend she is a whitegirl, one of the blond-haired ones, real American-looking. She is young and has her whole life ahead of her. She has a boyfriend in Sac and a bit of income. It isn't so bad. She could become an actress, or a dancer. But what she'd really like to do is work the counter at Woolworth's, then settle down to have a family—lots of little towheaded babies.

Is this what they think of, lying in bed at night in the attic of a brothel? Of towheaded children in damp diapers? Poppy closes her eyes and concentrates a little more. She focuses on the body scent in the sheets and the pillow. This is Chloe's bed. Poppy focuses a little harder. She tries to see past the spinning in her head.

First, there is a coyote nuzzling fallen pears in the orchard. Poppy feels the wind ruffling its coat. It feels free—gentle enough to hold a pear in its iron jaws without bruising it, but strong enough to barrel through fences. On the other side of the fence is a road, and it walks along this road for miles, until a city comes into view. All its thoughts focus on leaving. Poppy covers her mouth to muffle a small burp. She's not going deep enough—these are mere dreams, their residue left on Chloe's pillow. She wants to know what Chloe desires, what she thinks in her conscious mind.

Richard bucks on top of her and she squeezes her eyes shut and measures her breath. She keeps the fear down in her chest, reminds herself to keep from clenching her thighs. She smells the waxy pomade in his hair and the curls of heat and sweat that rise off his stomach with each thrust. Richard brings her arm up around his neck. His sleek shoulder and the ripple of muscle make her hand tingle. Chloe hates it! The realization startles Poppy's eyes open. She'd been convinced it was a love affair, with some coyness on Chloe's part. She turns her face into the pillow. Beneath the hate—neediness, dependence. After the sex, there will be money, and after the money, an apartment in the city, maybe a shopgirl job at a department store. There'll be café dinners after work with the other girls, nights on the town. Rides to the top floors of hotels where she can look out on building after building that break the sky. There'll be the drum of pounding jackhammers, men who speak different languages slamming bolts into metal structures, and bakeries whose scents are lost in the smell of fresh tar. If Poppy tries a little harder, she's sure she'll know Chloe's future. She finds a strand of Chloe's blond hair on the pillowcase.

She won't marry, as she is attracted only to men who are guaranteed to leave. She won't ever have children. Her mother will die before she can see her again and her brother will forget her. Poppy pushes sickness back in her throat, convinces herself she doesn't smell like gin. Her father has gone mad with guilt and he dies a wanderer who lives off the kind hand of the city. She will learn loneliness by growing old in an apartment without mementos, where her life is lived through a glowing blue screen that flickers to her the outside world. The violence of the gangsters spreads west, until even children have guns. The diamond window magnifies the light, which has risen to noon brilliance. Poppy begins to cry, miserable, dizzy, ready to vomit. The house is so quiet. She needs sounds to break with the afternoon light, so that she knows that it really is Chloe's lonely future she sees and not her own.

24

TWO GIRLS WALK down Main Street on another bright day. The air is heavy and wet, like a room after the wash has just been done, when the steam clouds the window that gives a glimpse of the lawn. People are sweaty and noisy, squinting and calling for rain. The boats horn down the river. The girl with the uneven red-brown hair is looking for her father, but she makes an adventure of it. She dawdles, stops to look at the lone rose rising up between two buildings toward sunlight, reads the window ads, ponders what kind of person she will be if she buys this brand of cigarettes or that.

Coming the other way is the blonde with the timid eyes. She carries ice cream in a paper bag. Her steps are direct. One can tell she's the girl who never outgrew her baby fat, who has elegant tapered fingers, but a paunch-stomach. She catches sight of the brown-haired girl looking in the store window, and she pauses. She is almost home; it would be silly to cross the street.

The brown-haired girl turns from the window. She is looking for her father. He is not at this end; he may be at the other. She gazes down the street, and over the shoulders and in between the spaces of passersby who move in and out of the light slanting between the balconies that cover the sidewalk, she sees the blonde, frozen, clutching a paper bag. She looks at the store window, and across the street, then starts walking again. She must find her father. She smiles. The crowd may jostle her, she may be nudged to the side, and the collision with the blonde will be unavoidable.

The two girls on Main Street are walking toward one another.

They pass, brush, cloth across skin, sleeve of one against the arm of the other. Waves and salt-foam billow out between. It's the illicit that attracts them—nighttime meetings, looks sneaked in the street, swimming beyond the trees—and this is the zenith moment: the barely-there touch on a busy street at high noon.

25

BEFORE CHLOE CAN see Sofia, there is the church. A small lantern glows on the floor. The two women sit on either side, the inconstant light sending up haggish shadows. They nest in humped blankets. Chloe brushes flakes of windowsill paint from her fingers and pushes through the front door.

The boat-women are startled. They say nothing as she approaches.

With a sweep of her hand she asks if she can sit. She was sure they spoke only Chinese, but one says: Sit.

Chloe introduces herself. Go on telling your stories. I just want to listen.

We want to know about you. The younger one speaks. She has the face of an angel dancing atop a face-powder box. Tit for tat.

A story about me? Chloe asks. For a year at Madam See's, people have shown only mild interest in each other. It is enough they are there; no one wants to know why. Beatrice has a boyfriend; Lisel has a daughter; Julia has no one; but that is all. Thrown together, with no desire to forge something more intimate.

Tit for tat.

And I go first?

The older one nods. She could stir at a cauldron with that face. Thirty-five or so, with a broke-beak nose.

I'm seventeen. Chloe pulls a blanket up over her shoulders. This happened when I was fourteen. My daddy was kind of crazy from the war, so he didn't come home too much. And my mama worked late at the tomato cannery, so I had to put my brother David to bed. He was little, just nine, so he slept well, but I couldn't fall asleep. I used to stare out the bedroom window and watch the people passing by. Our house fell on the path to a speakeasy and you never saw so many drunks in your life. This night, a moaning brought my eye to the road. A woman had fallen in the mud. She kept trying to push herself up, cursing goddamn. Then she stopped. I was reluctant to go out there, but I was afraid she'd suffocate in the mud. I put on my coat and went out. The mud sucked at my shoes, nearly pulled them off.

Her dress had gotten hitched up. She had mud all over her wool stockings. She looked like a beast. I was afraid to touch her. I couldn't see her face, so I touched her neck. Her skin was cold, but I could feel some heat deep beneath. I pushed her shoulder. She turned and her mouth was marked up with vomit. I wanted to cry, because that was my mama.

My mama, who never talked much, save to say do the wash or wipe down the table or boys'll bring you trouble or shhhh sleep baby. I just kept calling her until she roused. I had to pull her skirt down. I said all the nonsense things she said to my brother when he woke from night terrors until she got up and I walked her through that nasty mud and to bed.

The women say nothing. Now your story? Chloe asks, embarrassed by their silence. Maybe people don't have drunk mothers in China.

No wonder you're a whore, says witch-face. Just look at your mother.

Chloe surprises herself. Is that the story she would tell them if she was brave enough to burst into the church and demand their confidence? She flicks one pebble toward Sofia's window, but Sofia comes through the kitchen door.

Pear orchard? Chloe asks. Her anxiety over her story fades under giddiness. She didn't need the pebble; Sofia was waiting.

EGRETS FLUTTER UP and down from the treetops with the sound of rippled canvas. They flash wary eyes at the two girls sitting at the trunk of a fruit-bare tree. Chloe brushes her palm against Sofia's ragged hair and tells her she likes it short. Sofia pushes smoke through her teeth. It fans out messy.

What'd you do on the Fourth?

Saw a movie. Chloe almost tells her about seeing David, but Sofia would pry more.

Was it good?

It was okay. It was too hot to do anything else.

I'm sorry about Tuesday. Spilling all your wine and acting that way.

Chloe laughs. This quick forgiveness is a flaw. But Sofia is not Alfred, or any of them. It's too much to think about on such a clear night. Chloe says, Play with my hair? She puts her head in Sofia's lap. She squints off, trying to see past the trees into the darkness beyond. She wonders if the birds will fly away at the hint of a coyote. Will they be warned?

What are they like? Chloe asks.

Who?

Those women. What do they do? There's talk around town, but it's hard to tell who's seen them and who's making it up.

Chloe wants to know if they traveled across the sea on that tiny boat, eating fish they pulled from the ocean with their bare hands. And she wants to know what they do now, in the church, or in the living room, in the heat behind closed curtains.

Sofia snorts. They're very boring. Mama and Baba are always helping people, giving them a place to stay. Sai Fung and So Wai aren't any different.

But Chloe still thinks of the boat and escape by water. She tucks some hair behind her ear. Sofia pulls it out again and runs her fingers along the strands. I want to tell you something, Chloe says. When I got to Madam See's, they didn't make me work right away. I mean not in that way. First I had to stay in this small room. Downstairs. It had a small window and the men who couldn't pay a lot, you know, could pay a little and I'd open the curtain and they could look at me.

They paid just to look? The smoke has stopped.

Not exactly. I'd do whatever they wanted me to, but they couldn't touch me.

Has my father ever come in?

I don't know.

You've never seen him?

I've never seen him. But Chloe can't be sure. All of the men of town have passed through Madam See's door—the pious and the unsaved.

I feel sorry for you, Chloe.

Chloe sits up and pulls away from Sofia's fingertips. Don't feel sorry for me. I'm going to leave soon. It's a plan that emerges suddenly, against Sofia's sympathy. Her pity is far removed from the reality of Chloe's life within those red walls. To Sofia it must be all abstract notions, and Chloe can't convey the breath and the stickiness and the eyes that you can't (must not must not) open, because seeing is the only sense you can stop. You know Lisel? She's over fifty—she has kids and everything. She's going to be there until she dies. Chloe spits the words.

Where will you go?

I don't know. Sacramento. Wherever I can, with whatever money I have.

Sofia brings up one knee and picks at a scab. I'll miss you.

Foreign words to Chloe, who has never been told this: I will miss you.

Sofia still concentrates on the crust on her knee. I'd go with you, Chloe. I'll leave with you.

Before Chloe answers, the sound of Sofia's name echoes through the trees. The startled egrets stretch their wings and lift up like incandescent sheets being shaken dry.

It's Mama, says Sofia.

SOFIA RUNS UP from the direction of the orchard.

Where have you been? That's trespassing, Corlissa hisses.

I didn't hop the fence. A little whine in her protest.

Corlissa leans forward and sniffs as her daughter speaks. Sofia shrugs her face away.

You smell like cigarettes.

I was chewing on a piece of grass.

Corlissa almost laughs. She breathes hard to keep from slapping her. Get upstairs and brush your teeth. Sofia clears her throat. She looks her straight in the eye, then drops her head and runs inside.

Corlissa remains on the lawn, arms folded against the cold, searching out the shape of the orchard fence. She would like to say, Wait until your father hears about this, but Howar is away, looking for the women's families and papers, and when he returns, she knows the urgency of the event will have been lost. She thinks of straps and switches and the red welts her own mother left on the backs of her thighs. She had always deserved it. Sofia deserves it. She centers her anger until she feels she can direct it into a swinging arm, a hand clutching her husband's belt. She thought that once Sofia was a teenager, spanking would be undignified, that the girl could be reasoned with. But the look straight in the eye, the repeated warnings, the threats! Sofia is a completely unreasonable creature, who seems to know only through her skin.

Something flashes at the orchard fence. A boy? Had Sofia gone off with a boy? She takes a few steps closer, to the edge of the church lawn where the grass meets the gravel. The figure moves toward Main Street. Corlissa crosses the road and walks up between the two houses that face the church. She'll take the alley route, cut the person off.

She stoops under the lit windows of her neighbors. She's ashamed to have not known earlier, all along, that it has been this. A prank letter received last week, tossed in among peelings and other trash, warned her of this. Anonymously written, misspelled words. With cruelty, the letter had mentioned a girl and Corlissa was confused. Unfathomable and impossible. She lingers in the alley to wait for the boy to pass. Her heart beats fast. She is sweating. Her hair has loosened from its bun and is hot and heavy on her neck.

She waits, but no boy passes. She peeks out to Main. The only person there, now turning toward the brothel, is a whitegirl, one of the prostitutes. Corlissa steps onto the road and walks back down toward the orchard. To the left, the levee road is empty, and on the right, the orchard fence is bare. The boy has disappeared. A fear pushes up and Corlissa pushes it down, a constant play between her thumping heart and her rising hope. Maybe it wasn't a boy. The thought turns for a second. No. Where did he go?

26

TUFFY LEAMON'S SPEAKEASY has run dry. The crops are rotting in the fields. Revelry is the only thing men want. One Sunday, Howar gives a sermon that quotes the Song of Songs. The men, turning back to their Bibles, find revelation in learning newfound words:

> Thy cheeks are comely with ornaments, thy neck with
> strings of jewels. We will make thee plaits of gold with
> studs of silver.

The next day, all the jewelry to be found or bought in town has been left on Howar and Corlissa's doorstep. Howar's new congregation is testing him; he tacks a sign to the door:

EXODUS 20:15:
    The Eighth Commandment: Thou shall not steal.

He intends it to be stern in its brevity. The few wives in town show up to claim their missing pieces. They pick out their belongings from the glittering baubles laid out on the dining room table.

Another week, another batch of jewelry. Howar posts a new note:

> EPHESIANS 4:28: Let him that stole steal no more: but rather let him labor, working with his hands the thing which is good, that he may have to give to him that needeth.

The wives return again for their jewelry. At home, the rubies and rhinestones and dark yellow gold are locked inside of a box locked inside another box and hidden under the sink, or on the top shelf of the closet, behind the hatbox. But even the women know it is futile against the desperation of lovesick men.

After his table is bare, every ring and bracelet and hairpin and necklace returned to its owner, Howar finds a note lying at his front door. It looks as if it has drifted here—carefully written, starting to curl, without an envelope and unsigned.

> *Brother Lee,*
> *Song of Songs 8:7: Many waters cannot quench love, neither can the floods drown it: if a man would give all the substance of his house for love, it would be utterly contemned.*

27

BETWEEN THE HABERDASHERY and Locke's oldest
building is a restaurant with a dance floor on the second
level. It has wood floors, waxed and treated to minimize the
half-moons and nicks left by dancing heels. Chloe finds herself there more often. Richard has not been by in a week, and
Chloe must pay her room and board to Madam See.

She starts with a smile and a glance away. The men are surprised to see a whitegirl so coy. They scoot nearer to her chair.
She watches the dancers, but there are always little looks to
the men to make sure she has not lost their attention. Sometimes they are not Chinese. In the evenings, the revelry opens
to everyone and she finds herself talking to Japanese, Filipi-
nos, and whites.

The other girls guide her, because she's never had to hustle
before. Julia leans over and tells Chloe she'd better stand up
and dance. Not only that, she'd better grab a guy and pull him
in. She'd better flaunt herself.

Chloe dislikes being the center of attention, but she loves
to dance. She eases herself into the dance floor crowd and

begins to show off what she learned in New York. She spins and stamps until she's lost in the furious noises of men going mad with the passion of music-making; the insistent thrum of a bassist's finger and the pluck of a guitar. The horns wail their piece too. Every one of them, she thinks, has sold his soul to the devil at the crossroads. The pomade in her hair gets warm, her curls come loose, and her body gets damp.

Her hips nudge against other dancers. The attention that was once on her and her stylish moves shifts away; she is part of the crowd. Chloe delights in the anonymity, especially as Julia's hoots and shrieks draw the looks away. I can't dance! Julia exclaims and laughs as a man grabs her and spins her and leads the way. It is just Chloe dancing, alone, eyes closed in a rising euphoria of hot bodies and loud music and the ground thumping beneath with the movements of a hundred feet. She wants to clasp this one moment of joy and not think of what comes next: a man too impatient to make it inside the brothel, tumbling under the levee-side porch, Chloe crying because her dress'll be ruined in the dirt, and she had to pay three dollars for it out of the Bernard-Hewitt catalog. She closes her fist a little tighter and keeps dancing.

28

PASSING BY, RICHARD hears about Chloe's tumble beneath the porch. He stops, tips his head: What? The laughing men, gathered at the back of the Lucky Fortune to smoke, muffle their snickers, concentrate on their cigarettes. Even the man who has been drawn in from his bench seat returns to perusing the newspaper.

What did you say? Richard asks. He turns to Manny, who shouldn't be in there anyway. He should be in the alley, giving the last kick to poor losing saps. Manny hocks into the spittoon. Chloe. Last night. A snicker catches in someone's nose, but Manny does not smile.

The anger swells up with such force that Richard coughs before he speaks: The problem with this town is that no one has anything better to do than gossip.

It's clear you've had your hands full, says Arthur Sun. The cool voice, the way he glances off to the side when he exhales smoke—this man has suckled Chloe's breasts and seen the shimmer-line of hair that leads from belly button down. Richard wants to throw himself on Arthur, knock the cigarette from his hand, break the smirk from his face. But the others would be upon him in an instant, pulling at his suit and urging calm. This would give him no satisfaction, so he goes to find Chloe.

POPPY JUMPS WHEN he slams the door. He locks it. She smiles a little, stops.

You're not here to say you love me. She turns back to her work. Richard swipes his hands across her desk and her books are on the floor, bindings humped, pages bent, edges dust-marked.

What are you doing? She acts as if outraged men lock themselves in her office everyday. She takes a pack of cigarettes out of her drawer and taps one out. I'd offer you one, but with that sort of behavior... She lights her cigarette.

What are you doing? He shoots the question back to her.

One must hold up his end for the other to hold up hers. Chloe has bills to pay.

He kicks a book. You're not fair, Poppy.

He watches her face for some revelation. She's beautiful— tiny lines by her eyes like crackled porcelain, a pert mouth and indifferent black eyes—but too cold to be attractive. Chloe chooses how she pays her bills, Poppy says. I just collect the rent. Talk to her.

He leaves the office. George is on his heels, stuttering: Mr. Fong, s-stop. You can't go up there. Then Poppy's voice floats out of the office like a salvation, Goddammit, George, let him go.

CHLOE BACKS HERSELF against the bed. Richard clenches his fists. He brings his hand up to his mouth and coughs. His heart has never beat like this. His stomach wrenches in happy anticipation of a fight. Chloe's eyes are wide and blue and unfazed. Why does everyone refuse to be startled by him today?

He kicks the nightstand. This is thank you? He kicks the nightstand. This, this is thank you? The drawer cracks and falls askew.

Madam See will make you pay for that. He detects a tattletale rise and fall in her voice.

Richard slams his fist on top of the nightstand. The wood caves. I paid for this! I'll break whatever I want! The pain feels good, cuts into the passion poisoning his blood.

Richard, calm down. A quiver of crying in her voice, but no apology. His hand sweeps the vase to the floor. The shatter pops like breaking bones.

Why can't you say you're sorry? Aren't you sorry? He coughs. He tears the curtains from the rod. He stumbles backward, out of the way of the dowel that swings free from its bolts. The red gauze still clenched in his hands. Back to the window. He hefts it open with one hand and lets free the curtains. They drift toward the ground, then snag, hanging off the building in a frayed wrinkle of red.

Chloe scoots herself against the headboard and brings her knees to her chest. What was I supposed to do? What did you want me to do? She begins to cry, but the remorse comes too late.

He leaps onto the bed. Through her hiccups and crying, she pleads, Stop it stop it stop it. She crosses her arms in front of her face. Richard pulls at her arms with one hand and grabs her hair with the other. He smacks her face. Chloe screams. Richard throws himself on top of her, yanks her head toward him, and, not knowing quite what else to do, bites her neck. She tears at his hair and tries to knee him away. When he tastes blood, the whirlwind of all the minutes, the blankness of his mind, clears. He releases her. The poison subsides. He moves to the end of the bed, coughing. Everything's been released in the press of teeth on tendons. The circle of bloody teeth marks on Chloe's neck starts to bruise. Richard's hands shake. Chloe curls up and cries quietly.

He stands up. Sweat pinpricks his forehead. Compared to blind blank fury, his mind feels full and chaotic and phlegm clots his chest. He looks around the destroyed room.

He says over and over, I'm sorry, I'm sorry. He leaves the room. George and Poppy are not waiting outside with reprimands. He swallows and waits for the taste of Chloe's blood to leave his mouth.

AFTER MADAM SEE leaves the room, broken vase carried in a dustpan, Chloe's fingers lift up to touch the tenderness of her cheek. She takes a mirror from the splintered drawer and looks at the bruise that cradles her eye like a split plum. Her lids are not swollen, thank goodness, the eye unharmed and protected by bone. She tips her head and looks at her neck. Splotchy red and adorned with two facing crescents of broken skin. The bite is not deep—just enough to scab a little, and to bruise around the scabs. She runs her fingers over it lightly. The marks are small and even.

She takes a deep breath and replaces the mirror. The drawer takes some jiggling to close and the splinters nip at her skin. It is the nipping, not the sight of her battered skin, that finally makes her cry again.

She wants to dig her nails into her flesh, grab hold and peel it back. She wants to shear away her hair, leaving bristles and white scalp behind. She wants to scrub at all the places where the world enters her body until they bleed and renew. She grabs her hair and presses back her screaming sobs. She kicks her feet against the bed. She doesn't want to leave home, or New York, or Madam See's, she realizes—she wants to leave herself.

The impossibility makes her cry harder. She turns and muffles her mouth in her pillow, bites hard on cotton and down. When she was ten, all she'd wanted to be was a school-teacher. She'd been diligent with her letters, with her math, but could never rise beyond being a mediocre student. This she had not imagined. She wonders if any woman in Madam See's had—no, this was the alternate future, the life that tumbles down when being a nurse or a schoolteacher or a secretary or a shopgirl fails.

Whore. Chloe whispers the word to herself; it's the first time she's let it come off her tongue. I'm a whore. It startles her to speak it. The words linger in the broken red room, their presence suddenly transforming the room from a romance of brocade wallpaper and lantern light into a contrived space where money is exchanged for her flesh. She touches her cheek and whimpers at the soreness.

Her skin tingles as her tears subside—all the discrete moments of the past two years come together into a stomach flutter, a quickening heartbeat. Her back on the cold tile floor in New York, belly rising six months fat. Alfred turning her away in San Francisco. Her brother in the movie theater, and then her swaggering promise to Sofia that she will step out of this town just as she stepped out of her own two years ago. The twinges of intuition gather, shape themselves as coherent words in her mind. She must leave Locke. She will leave Locke.

IT WAS ONLY a dime-store vase, milky white and adorned with Mediterranean-blue flowers that bloomed around the circumference. But the clatter of the shards into the trash made Poppy cringe, and so she finds herself knocking on Richard's door. She hears shuffling inside. She knocks again and Richard answers.

When he had left the brothel, she'd not noticed how haggard he looks. He stands in the doorway now with thin sagged shoulders, a pale tint to his lips. He coughs into his shoulder, rubs his mouth against the angular joint, and says, I'm sorry, Poppy. His face is expressionless and the smears of darkness under his eyes seem to draw them down. With such blankness in his voice, how can she be sure of his sincerity?

What were you—

Please, can we talk about this later?

No. Let me in.

My wife, he says in English.

I don't care. She pushes gently against the door. It nudges past Richard, then swings open. Richard sighs and looks to the couch.

His wife sits there, looking at Poppy. Ming Wai. Poppy's memories of her face from the day of the Dragon Boat Festival are not too clear and now it is like seeing her again for the first time. She is small—smaller than Poppy, even—with a thin, compact body. The darkness of her eyes seeps from corner to corner, the whites barely visible. And her complexion—cast in blue like skin on boiled milk. Poppy cannot speak.

And then there is the smell. Poppy purses her mouth. On the surface, it is the smell of a small apartment lived in for days by two people without a fan or an open window. Every breath that leaves the body contained in a few rooms until pore-stench, lung-stench, and shit smell combine. Below this, heightened by Poppy's senses, it's the smell of the dead stealing from the living—the way a decaying corpse can poison a river or a house. Richard brings his fist up to his mouth, coughs, and says, Come in if you must come in.

Ming Wai challenges Poppy with her eyes. Though she is small, she sits as if she owns the couch. As if she owns the card table that sits off to the left, the short shelf of knickknacks out of sight that Poppy remembers from her only visit, the nubs of stained carpet. Poppy realizes there is more at stake than Chloe's bruised face or Richard's bad behavior. Poppy's dreams and panic, she is now sure, lead back to this source— to this apartment and to this woman. Is Ming Wai there, but not there? With the heaviness of a body but the ephemerality of a spirit?

Poppy drops her gaze. I'm sorry, Richard. I won't bother you. I must go.

Richard clears his throat and nods as he eases the door shut.

Poppy turns away to face the sun.

29

The River Ghost (1910)

A WHOOP AROSE from the riverside. Not a yell of joy, but of alarm and warning that caused Po Pei to stop tossing stones and look in the direction of the river. Houses obscured her view, but she saw her neighbor, Old Chan, run past the field with the soles of his shoes flopping, followed by a pack of dirty-faced children. Po Pei stood stork-still to watch them pass, caught up in the swirl of kicked-up dust and excited cries.

Girl, what are you doing? her father yelled from a few rows over. His shoulder muscles tensed under the strain of the plow. She glanced at him, then stooped to find more stones, moving slowly so as to untangle the commotion of sound that wound from the river, around houses, and to her father's turnip field. The sun was hot on the back of her neck and burned through her thin cotton shirt. She swiped her arm against her sweaty forehead. Dirt had crept into the crack of a broken toenail and stung. The voices at the water grew more insistent, broken up by the oohs and aahs of children.

The whole field seemed to be stone-filled. Po Pei wondered where they came from each planting season, because she was sure she'd cleared them all away the year before. She brushed her dirty hands on her pants. How could she get to the river? She tried to swallow with a dry mouth and felt the tightness in her throat.

Ba, I'm going for water, she shouted. He looked at the expanse of rock-cleared soil between the two of them and nodded.

She walked slowly to the house. Against the east wall, she leaned to unroll her pant cuffs and shook out the dirt. When she rounded the corner, out of sight from her father, she broke into a run to the river. She glanced from side to side into the round courtyard doorways of her neighbors, glided past walls made of packed mud and straw. She held her breath as she skipped by the henhouse to avoid its hot, feathery scent. Finally she broke through the winding dirt alleys and approached the waterfront.

There were three men waist deep, struggling with something large in the water. Old Chan, Po Pei's neighbor, stood close by. He tried to ease forward to help, but there was room only for three and he inched back, stepped from side to side, and tried to be useful. The children, elbow-high to Po Pei, clung to each other on the shore, occasionally turning their faces into another's shoulder, or stamping giddy feet and crying out.

What's going on? she asked them.

They found a woman, one answered.

Some sampans gathered, steadied in the water by long

poles. The observers left an arc of space around the men, their faces were grim, and one could nearly make out the squint of disapproval.

One of the men turned away with a scowl, brought his hand to his face, and covered his nose and mouth. Then, with a breath, back to the body. Another man, shirtless, backed up onto the shore, dragging two swollen legs. The other two held her arms. Old Chan followed them out of the water, saying, Gently, gently.

Po Pei stepped forward. She tried to peek beyond the men's shoulders and saw only the gleam of their skin. She stepped forward again, four paces, and finally she could see through the space between their bodies.

The woman was so bloated that her skin shone. The lace of algae across her face further obscured her identity. Was it an accident? the people asked one another. They didn't utter the other possibility. This alternative fascinated Po Pei. Not murder, but suicide arising out of a scandal. She had heard that in other villages unfaithful women were bundled up in baskets like pigs and tossed into the water. She'd never seen the punishment herself, and in most cases the offending woman drowned herself first to save face. Fifteen years old and feeling the first ripples of passion, Po Pei realized yet another motivation. Perhaps the women killed themselves not to save face, but out of passion, out of frustrated desire. Po Pei tried to move even closer.

The woman's wrist had swollen around and nearly hidden

a thin jade bracelet. Old Chan saw it and cried out his wife's name. She went to see her mother, he explained, three days ago. He grimaced, as if he wanted to hold the body, but couldn't bring himself to. Instead he pulled stones from the pockets of her torn coat.

See Po Pei! She turned at the sound of her father's angry voice calling her name. The men gathered around the body looked up and the children snickered. Worthless girl! I should trade you for a bag of rice! Better yet, I'll sell you to America. He grabbed her arm. Po Pei tipped her head and blushed as the children laughed. When I'm done whipping her, I'll come back for you, her father shouted at the children. They shrieked and giggled as they tried to hide behind each other.

Po Pei's father began to pull her away, but her feet resisted and dragged in the sand. He stopped and followed her eyes to the body. His loosening fingers caught her attention. In his face, there was a glancing recognition and the shimmer of a hundred other things. She watched him and tried to tease out the meaning of his expression. Old Chan's wife was twenty-six, and had not yet had children. She smiled too easily, Po Pei's mother had complained, but her father never seemed to mind. Old Chan was much older; she was his second wife, and he had grown children in other villages. She didn't slip, despite what Old Chan muttered over and over. She threw herself. Her father's nostrils flared. He remembered himself, yanked Po Pei away. As they walked quickly toward the field, he pressed his mouth to her ear and said, That is what happens to women who don't obey.

They took water from the bucket—warm minerally water that dribbled from the ladle down their chins—then went back to the field. Her father resumed at the plow and Po Pei scanned the ground for stones. The skin on her neck and back was tender—sunburnt, she knew. Her lower back ached; her arms were sore. She tipped her head up, to look out from under her hat, and saw her father. He had paused at the plow, his face bent into his arm. His shoulders shook.

Ba? she yelled.

He lifted his head and looked at her. She was too far to see his face. He waved his hand to her, then straightened up and began pushing again. Po Pei reached the end of the field, removed what she believed was the last rock. She went to wash the dirt from under her nails. From the pan where she washed, she gazed across to her father. He was a mere outline against the red sky, still plowing.

THE GHOST CAME the next week. Po Pei first saw her in the well. At first glance, her own reflection, but as she peered over to lower the bucket, she saw it was the face of her neighbor, Old Chan's wife. The bucket broke the reflection, until it was merely ripples of the sun overhead. ,

Po Pei began to see Old Chan's wife in every water surface—her cup as she tipped to drink, the water she bathed in, the trough where the animals drank. Her mother would say it was Po Pei's imagination, but Po Pei was sure it was a water ghost. If she could sense the future, why not also the world not on the other side of time, but the other side of the veil? Those who were neither living nor dead, but in limbo for unfulfilled destinies, or to gain retribution. Po Pei was nervous, but not afraid. In the far side of the field, she burned money for the dead, and watched as the wind swept in and carried the ashes up into the sky, up to heaven.

She awakened one night to her mother's angry voice in the loft above. She lifted her head from her pillow, just a bit, and held herself very still, holding even her breath. Her mother had seen Old Chan's wife and she was asking her father why. Why did the ghost linger here rather than at Chan's? What did she want with them? Her father said, over and over, I don't know, I don't know and his murmur was broken by a thud and the sound of liquid. The chamber pot next to Po Pei's bed had overturned and spilled. Urine narrowed from a puddle into a stream, stopped at the ladder, pointing like an accusing finger.

Po Pei? her mother asked.

It wasn't me, Mama, Po Pei, in fear, admitted. It was a ghost. And she told her mother how she had seen Old Chan's wife everywhere, for the last few days. Her mother listened quietly. When Po Pei was finished, she screamed at Po Pei's father, because there was only one explanation for the lingering spirit.

The next afternoon, Po Pei's mother returned from the medium with three pieces of paper, marked with characters and threaded with gold leaf. Her mother instructed each of them to dip the paper in their tea and rub it on their faces and necks. Then she burned the paper and mixed the ashes into their tea. The taste and texture made Po Pei gag, but the ashes would protect them. Her father drank it without comment, with downcast eyes.

Rather than disappearing, the ghost seemed to multiply. She moved from water surfaces to glass so that Po Pei saw her through every window. According to the old stories, the ghost wouldn't be settled until she gained retribution, but Po Pei couldn't reconcile her sightings with the stories. She looked in on rooms where the ghost cooked, embroidered, swept, plucked chickens. When Po Pei burst into these rooms, determined to catch the ghost unaware, there was no one, save for a last floating feather, or a settling cloud of swept dust.

Her father began to work more slowly, to move deliberately. Po Pei thought it was guilt—his face paling, his body narrowing. Her mother, content with the eaten ashes, did not notice. One night when they had all been sleeping for hours and a chill had fallen on the room, Po Pei saw her father climb down the ladder and slink out the front door. Caught up in the world of old stories, where the daughter trails her sneaking-away father to discover secrets, she followed him.

He was careful with his feet. He did not let his soles lift too high above the ground, did not let them slap back down, so that he glided through the village, past dark windows and settled animals. Po Pei followed him to the cemetery on the hill. At a grave whose stone glowed pink in the moonlight, he met a woman. The woman was clean and light as polished ivory, her clothes pressed and beautiful, but Po Pei could see it was Old Chan's dead wife. Under the deception of the moon, her face was carefree, joyful. They embraced, and even in the small touch, Po Pei saw the transference of her father's essence. He grew dimmer as the woman shone. He was losing his yang chi'i, his male essence, his life-light. His yin had grown unbalanced—too much darkness, too much moon, too much female.

The next morning, her father couldn't even rise from bed. Her mother cursed him and fed him soup in a single gesture; it was love tempered by annoyance. Po Pei opened her mouth to tell her mother—It's more than a fever!—and felt her breath being sucked away, every gasp she took to form the words stolen and her mouth filled with ice. Her mother shouted at her to not stare with her mouth agape like some village idiot. Po Pei clamped down on the iciness and didn't dare to speak.

With a closed mouth, Po Pei gathered up all she knew from the old tales and decided on a remedy of her own. She got large bundles of hell notes—sacrificial money for the dead—and crept into her neighbor's henhouse. Inside, the light was dusty, fell through the spaces between the warped wood, but was enough to reflect back the glitter of a hundred small eyes. Po Pei moved slowly, choosing carefully. Most of the birds rose up and fluttered away from her with a squawk, so she grabbed for the one that was too slow, too weak, that only shivered on its roost at her approach.

Again, at the far side of the field, Po Pei burned the hell notes. The chicken squirmed on the ground, its legs bound. As she threw more money onto the pile, Po Pei saw the ghost approach, drawn by the lure of underworld wealth. She came closer, cautiously, as if she could not believe all this money was for her. When the ghost was within a few feet, her eyes caught on the swirling rising money-ash, Po Pei sliced the chicken's neck and held it upside down. It convulsed with more vigor than it ever held in life. The ghost looked from the ash to the blood draining onto the ground, and her mouth opened in shock. She turned to leave, but the vacuum left by the hen's escaping soul sucked in the wandering ghost. Poppy turned the hen right-side up, and bandaged the slit on its neck. It clucked weakly. It was no longer a chicken, but a vessel for the ghost of a slighted lover.

Po Pei kept the hen as a pet; she had to ensure that it did not die before the ghost was firmly entrenched as a chicken spirit. It clucked around their doorway, cocked its head at her recovering father, and occasionally leaped into a fit of feathers and dust, as if trying to escape itself. It scurried from her mother, and pecked at Po Pei's feet. By the time her father glowed again with his balanced yin-yang, when the dark half-moons were gone from under his eyes, the chicken settled into itself. It was as meek as it was in the beginning, too languid to do more than roost, too shy even to lay eggs. In this state, Po Pei returned it to the henhouse.

30

THE PIG WRITHES and kicks and cries as they wrestle it off its feet. They slice its throat. The blood spurts and runs over its eyes. Chloe watches the body drain; the squeals fade to snorts, then silence. The white-aproned men move in the artificial light and cast long shadows as they slice open the pig and clean it. Dark spreading blood stains the starched whiteness. The smell of offal taints the nightly ritual, a reminder of the pigs jostling in the barn just yards away. Smoke pipes from the pit and coals hum red at the bottom. The men wrestle the pig onto a spit and lower it into the ground. The baking begins near midnight. By morning the pig will be roasted and ready for market.

Chloe rounds the barn and catches sight of herself in a mirror that dangles from an eave. She's not sure if it's a talisman to thwart angry pig ghosts, or a mere convenience for the men who spend so much time here that they shave with this mirror steadied in one hand and a dry razor in the other. Green streaked with yellow cups her eye like a bloom. Richard's bite is scabbed and faint. She'll just have to go to Sofia looking like a rumpled alley cat.

At the Hangman's Tree, Sofia curls into the trunk, her

knees up. She's smoking again, looking slightly ridiculous—a child's round face, with the cigarette held between her tiny pink lips. Despite all her city-girl aspirations, she blends into the landscape as a sneaking-out country girl in a dirty dress and shoes ready for tromping through weeds. With her free hand, she touches Chloe's bruise.

Everybody has a need to pet bruises, Chloe says. She turns away.

What happened? Sofia flicks ash onto the dust at the roots. Chloe nestles against the tree and takes a deep breath. I didn't bring you anything.

I don't want anything from you or him. Especially from him. Richard. Sofia crushes the cigarette into the ground. What happened? A big-sister protectiveness comes through with her indignant set mouth. All this moving back and forth, flirtation, friendship enclosed in thin glass, now smashed. If Chloe has to say it all aloud, she'll cry.

Nothing, she whispers. Her brother in the theater, smiling like a stranger. If she doesn't tell Sofia, then who does she have? Chloe babbles about the slamming door, the broken drawers, the shattered vase, the biting. Quelled fear erupts. In Sofia's face, the glass is pieced back together. Chloe is fragile and downtrodden and pitiful. But somehow Sofia manages to say, Don't cry, Chloe. Chloe, Chloe. Don't cry.

Chloe lifts her head. Sofia places motherly lips on Chloe's tears. Chloe stiffens. Sofia pulls away and licks the salt from her lips. Don't cry.

Chloe hasn't known that there could be protection and caring woven through the lust and she wants to scream out curses from the wonder of it. Again, Sofia puts her mouth to Chloe's cheek and kisses at the tears. Does she dare? Her heart explodes with a different sort of fear. She turns her head. Her mouth finds Sofia's.

POPPY MUST BE systematic. She starts from the beginning, running through the narrative as she slips into a sweater. They had come on a cloudy day. No, it had been sunny, but clouded over just as the boat knocked toward shore. She slips on a man's hat—left in a room by someone who never reclaimed it—to shadow her face.

Downstairs, George leans in the doorway, sketching Celestials in longboats emerging from dark-lined clouds. In a finished sketch beneath them, two Immortals hunch over a wide tree stump, playing Go before the astonished eyes of a woodcutter. Poppy gently touches his shoulder.

Excuse me. She steps around him. I'll be back tonight.

George nods. He doesn't look up.

They came on a boat in the middle of unusual weather. Poppy repeats the story to herself. Out of a bank of fog. She tries to remember more as she steps down the alley and toward the slaughterhouse.

But she had fainted. Anything before the moment she saw them standing on land is only hearsay.

They've already killed the pig. A lantern glows in the corner of the yard. Beneath it, a man reads in a chair, with one eye on the cooking pig. His thoughts pass through her mind, shadows glimpsed behind a curtain. He is thinking of the book he reads, a sordid dime-store novel, and of a sore toe. The two thoughts are simultaneous. He looks up at the flicker of movement. Poppy raises a hand. He waves back. He only pretends to recognize her.

As she disappears into the weeds, footsteps over trampled grass, she feels the girls. She pauses, tries to listen. She closes her eyes, sees first a branch punched out like a fist, rope wrapped frayed, body hung, feet limp, and beneath, two heads pressed together, fingers streaking across tears, turning them to air. She wants the vision confirmed.

She breaks off the trail, crushes plants dried by the summer. She makes an arc around the front of the tree. Off to the side, she crouches and holds still. A small hand brushing over blond hair, snarling itself in it. Chloe and the preacher's daughter. Poppy remembers back to the troupe. Yellow silk stripped away to reveal bare skin, the coal that rubbed off Sarah and marked Poppy's lips. She became a puppet for hours at a time. Occasionally, she'd slip; her eyes would meet those of a woman in the audience and in the glitter of eyes ready to strike, in the clenched mouth, Poppy realized she was nothing more than an apparition conjured up by heat. When the woman returned home, pulled off her earrings, walked around the bedroom in her underclothes—hanging this, folding that—paused to scratch a fleck of dirt off her sole, Poppy would be recalled, with shame, as only a whore with blank eyes and a heaving chest. The nature of the two girls beneath the tree is different. An aberration. This is a bit of information she will save for later, for another anonymous letter to the preacher's wife.

Poppy scrambles up, steps carefully across the railroad tracks, and edges her way to the water. They came out of fog, and when they landed, Richard's wife fell to her knees and cried. All three women had seemed unsure on land. She'd come across water too, and wobbled onto shore with a new name. Newly released from three weeks of questioning on Angel Island, Poppy (renamed from the tongue-twisting Po Pei by immigrant officials) was unprepared for the city she had thus far only longed for from across the bay. First, there was the bustle on the dock where her new husband was to meet her. People shouted out in various dialects and languages, calling for their landsmen in order to hustle them over to the appropriate tong. A man led away a drably dressed group of girls. She drank it all in: the smells of water and smoke and bodies that had been at sea for weeks; the city opening up to the sunshine as the fog receded. Poppy felt jostled and hot and excited. She was fifteen years old, in America—Gold Mountain (she laughs now)—waiting to meet the man with whom she would spend her life. She carried a single bag, and the best that she had managed for this special meeting was new shoes. They had remained wrapped in cotton deep in her bag the whole trip over. Her hair was brushed as sleekly as it could be. She stooped to rummage through her bag for a tiny vial of scented ointment, slipped to her by her mother as a parting gift. She rubbed the spicy scent on her neck, kept an eye out for the man from the black-and-white photo she had glimpsed for a few minutes, months ago, when the marriage was first brokered. All she remembered was the pomaded hair and the Western dress. Any of these men—the tong brothers lounging against the posts smoking, or the wrinkle-suited men leading women away—could be him. She heard her name called. These were the only words that made sense and she clung to them above the other voices. She turned her head, looked all around. Some men laughed and punched each other playfully. Their queues flopped out from under felt hats. Though the men were dressed like merchants, Poppy realized, they couldn't be much older than she. Again, her name, and she yelled, Here I am! See Po Pei!

He came from behind. He was older—as old as her father! He smiled with a flash of gold teeth. He asked how her voyage was, she replied fine, then he picked up her bag and began walking. She followed. The picture that she'd seen, she realized, was from years before.

Maybe the women were just as deceived. Maybe Ming Wai expected a twenty-eight-year-old, wealthy Richard to be waiting onshore with a smile, as if ten years had not passed, as if ten years had not aged him. Poppy pushes her way through vines to a small spread of wet bank. The boat has been turned into a fort, strung with beads and tinsel and marked up with colored chalk. A man's tie hangs lank as an improvised flag. She puts her hands on it, wanting all memory. She wants the other side of the fog, beyond the Delta. Her palms pressed to soft wood. Her cheek on worn white paint. A lifeboat, without markings. Maybe her ear will reveal what tides in the hollow, like sounds washing out of a seashell.

Nothing. Just hands marked with a child's drawings.

31

CHLOE CROUCHES IN the tub. She dips the washcloth in the cold water that puddles around her ankles. She starts with her most private places, washes her feet, scrubs knees, then thighs. She is still modest. She dips the washcloth again, squeezes traces of blood from it. She washes gently, careful not to rub raw what is already irritated. She winces a little.

The gleam of the faucet reflects her face. The baby-blue room takes on a copper sheen in the rounded reflection. Despite the distortion of color and shape, Chloe can see the yellow haze that surrounds her eye. It is fading, diminished already from purple to blue to green. At the bend of the spigot, her face looks extra wide at the center, tall at the forehead and chin. She makes a face at herself; it distracts for a minute from the tenderness between her legs.

She's no longer the darling of the brothel. She sells herself as commonly as anyone else, performs her work in one of the narrow rooms that line the hall. The rooms are seven by four—space enough for a step and a bed. There's a trash basket beneath the bed, a small corner shelf with towels and rubbers.

Chloe feels entombed there. The small high window does not allow enough breeze to cut the heat created by two writhing bodies, and she pants not for passion, but for lack of air.

Chloe sticks her tongue out at her reflection. She wrings the cloth in her cold wet hands. Some of the other women have lapsed in the practice. They've lost faith. Chloe shakes out the washcloth and hangs it on the rack. She rises and water runs down her legs. She steps from the tub and onto the rug, grabs a towel, and dries herself.

SHE WAITS FOR him on the bed. It is his first time, he says, so he wants to wash up. From the edge of the bed, she can extend her legs and rest her feet on the opposite wall. She presses her heels against the wood and counts her toes. There's a knock at the door. It opens slowly and the boy steps in. Her age—seventeen or so. A scruff of hair rising despite the smear of hair oil, wire-rimmed glasses and a sheepish grin. He scratches the side of his nose. When she greets him, he glances at the floor.

You ready? she asks. He nods. She unbuckles, unbuttons him. His white shirttails hang like accordions.

Want something? she asks.

He stands in only a shirt, pants at his ankles, and nods again. She grabs a rubber and slips it on. I like that blanket, he says. It's pretty. He touches her hair; it's almost an affection-ate gesture.

Please don't.

He shrugs a little. She leans back on the bed and casts an impatient eye at him. He straddles her on his knees.

She closes her eyes to the rose-yellow walls and tries to remember how many bones there are in the human body. Two hundred and six, she thinks it is. She names to herself all the major organs—is skin considered an organ? What about the tongue? He whimpers in her ear. Is it true that cows have four stomachs? She turns her face away from his mouth, so that his breath warms her hair and not her ear. A groan and then a collapse.

There's a trash basket under the bed, she says. Towels up there. She gestures toward the shelf. She sits up when he does and awkwardly tries to straighten the coverlet beneath her. He unrolls, wipes, and discards. He buttons and buckles.

Do I...? He hesitates.

Pay me.

He slips some bills from his pocket and hands them to her. Thank you, he says. If he had a hat, she knows, he'd tip it.

She nods. Shut the door on your way out if you will.

DURING THE HEAT of the day, the Yuen Chong turns off its lights. The shopgirl upstairs pulls the shades and opens the door. Downstairs, the refrigerator cases hum, even louder in the absence of the sound of the electric lights. Chloe tucks a curl behind her ear, lost in the pondering of goods. The shuff-

shuff of shoes down the aisle catches her attention. It is Sofia, jar of tan lozenges in hand. Chloe measures her escape.

They have not seen each other in weeks. The day after their kiss, Chloe sat at the side of the road selling pear seconds. Sofia had bounced by with a gaggle of kids on their way to swim under the packing shed. The group laughed, cast curses under their breath, sent thorns into Chloe's heart. Sofia averted her eyes. For two nights, she ignored Chloe's rattle of pebbles against her window, and the next thirteen nights Chloe was too hurt to try. Though Chloe swore she didn't care, she kept an ear cocked to town gossip, straining for a word about Sofia. The speakers sensed her desire, kept reticent, and Chloe's curiosity grew alongside her anger at Sofia. Sofia had disappeared from her life for fifteen days and Chloe struggles to remember the sense of her, of what it'd been like between them. Chloe heads for the milk case, but Sofia's pull is too strong and she glances back.

Sofia is looking at her. Embarrassment furrows her brow. Chloe knows speaking to her will bring Sofia further shame, so Chloe tries to save her the trouble. She walks away.

Sofia comes up behind her. Wait. Hi. Hello. I was just getting some lozenges; my throat's been killing me something awful. I think I picked up a cold at the tree. It was so damp. She talks fast. This is a friendly interaction; this is the conversation people make in grocery stores. Comments on the weather should come next.

Chloe won't yield. She just nods. She glazes her eyes, sets

her mouth, as if Sofia is just another man coming to her with money and insults. Sofia blushes. She can't stop talking.

Feels like it might be getting cooler. Mama got a new fan. It really cuts the heat. Helps sleeping.

Chloe nods again. A bit of advice tickles her tongue: You don't know how to love yet, only how to take. But Sofia doesn't deserve that much.

I need to pay for this. Excuse me. She walks past Sofia. A finger of space between them; they do not even brush shoulders.

32

THE MAN WHO carves characters into the dirt in unsent letters home squats barefoot, toenails red with dust. His carving stick is held still, one stroke away from the character for "me." His head hangs down. The dust swirls a little around him in the breeze, then settles.

Strange, Poppy thinks, and continues on. It is midday, but Main Street has gone still. No one is pumping gas at the pump in front of the Foon Hop Co. Grocery; there are no dogs loping between parked cars. No children run in and out of the Yuen Chong with candy or soda. Even the rumble of river traffic is gone. Poppy puts her hand on the back of her neck; the sun is already starting to burn.

The dominoes in front of the Men's Center have been scooped up and put away. The men on the bench stare toward the street. They do not glance at her. She is accustomed to being ignored.

Inside the center, the lanterns are burning, but the games of poker and pai gow have faded into old men sitting stiffly on stools and benches. The cards are laid out on the felt-top tables in front of them. The light cast by the Coleman lanterns makes the scene look like it was torn from a yellowing newspaper. Poppy is not sure what is happening, but she is reluctant to break the peace.

Happy sits on the phoenix-dragon bench. His pipe is propped on the table beside him. Smoke rises gently from it. His eyes, with irises that have gone blue like a baby's, seem to have drifted to another place. Poppy whispers, Uncle Happy? She sits next to him. She reaches across and taps the tobacco from his pipe and into an ashtray.

The teakettle wheezes lightly and its top rattles from the steam. She gets up and fiddles with the heat. She sits back down.

I want to talk to you, Uncle Happy, she says. He does not blink. She sighs. She takes his hand in hers and feels sadness emanating from his warm palm to hers. No images come to her, just heat-sense. Her chest feels weak and her breath flutters out like ribbons. There's a soft oomph! as her breath and ability to speak is taken from her. She holds on to Uncle Happy's hand, linked by sadness. She stays with him in the dim light.

AT FIRST, SHE cannot find the women's boat. She shuffles carefully from tree line to waterline, hoping to stub her toe against a fragment. As her eye becomes accustomed to the varying shades of brown, she finds it topsy-turvy. Only the very bottom of the hull emerges from the ground. It seems the children built sand towers, poured buckets of river water to make mud pies, and gradually the boat disappeared under collapsed dirt and sludgy ground. The tie flag is wound into the mud, with a tongue of tainted color exposed. Of course, she thinks, they've forgotten it. A toy can be fun for only so long.

For many years, she's felt sure of most everything. Even things she could not control, she could predict. Now she feels lost. The sight of the forgotten boat, which will fade into the ground like buried bones in a matter of months, gives her heart pangs. She has to grasp every nuance of memory or, she fears, she'll lose Richard and all the little claps of happiness that have flashed intermittently over the years.

When she was sixteen, she had visions of whitemen in boats as she threw out the night slop buckets. The stench of an evening's worth of cooling human waste made her think she was looking through the hills where boys grazed water buffalo, to the sea, to a history on the water, but two days later a man came to the village, promises folded like bills in his pocket. He wore city clothes and a hat.

A day later, he sat at the table with her father—a farmer who tended fields filled with more stones than turnips. Her mother boiled water in the shadows and cradled her newborn boy, his mouth suckling air. The man brought out a photo and laid it on the table. A laundry owner, he said, and slid the picture over to her father. Stiff-backed in black and white, dressed in Western clothing with cropped hair, unsmiling. A Gold Mountain man. And if you don't like him, the man said, patting his pocket, I have many more. All rich. All in need of a wife. He gave Poppy kind smiles.

At night, she heard her parents in the thin-planked loft above, her mother's insistent voice against her father's murmur. Then the patter of her mother's bare feet, the slide of a trunk—her dowry trunk, she knew—the creak of hinges. Her mother exclaimed as she threw gold jewelry jangling onto the bed. Her mother said it was an opportunity; her father said the man should pay them.

Thus it was negotiated: the man paid $250 U.S.—for them, a fortune. He said her husband would sponsor her trip to America. The gold went back into the dowry chest, saved as a gift for her brother's future wife. And Poppy's premonition—of whitemen, of boats, of a mountain made of gold—became truth.

Disembarking from the boat in her travel clothes to evenings spent gazing through the wire-covered detention barracks window, Poppy smiled. Old women scolded her, told her to cover up her big horse teeth, that no man wants a woman as brash as that. So Poppy smiled behind her hand. She was so overcome by the excitement, her premonitions failed her.

Her husband spoke beautiful words in complicated sentences. It was only later, locked into his flat, that her euphoria of travel subsided and the visions came blaring back to her. Nothing was legal; there'd be no ceremony.

Ignorance. Poppy climbs atop the bit of exposed hull. Her resting heels make half-moons in the dirt. Ducks play and skitter across the water. Only ignorance, those lapses when her visions went dark, has given her sun-streaks of joy.

Blindness struck again the day she met Richard. She was waiting for the herbalist to measure out her sugared ginger. The bell above the door rang. Richard walked to the counter and waited for the herbalist's attention. Richard said to Poppy in his still-water voice, Do you know any remedies for a cold?

There's chicken broth, of course. And if you're losing your voice, a beverage of boiled dried kumquats will work well.

Poppy laughed and Richard laughed too. It burst from him like a child's eruption of surprise. The way he maintained himself—his carefully coifed hair, cream skin, and pressed clothes—radiated the illusion of being handsome, and Poppy was not sure if she could see past all these delicate, intentional touches. He did not look like a man with a cold. She paid for her ginger and, before Richard could tell the herbalist what he needed, she touched his arm and told him he could visit two doors down. Her fingers on his arm, she saw nothing, just a wide dark future, full of possibilities. The herbalist politely ignored the exchange.

Now she sits atop the boat and knows there should be ideas and hunches shooting through her like spasms of pain. She wants to know why and how these women have turned the town upside down. It has to be more than their numbers. Sure there are twenty men or more for every one woman. But are men such beasts that the flow of town life should be jarred? The boat is a mere dumb piece of wood. She's ignorant again, but there's no relief.

33

CORLISSA DIPS A plate into a basin of cold water. Sofia is upstairs sleeping off an illness. She's been slightly feverish for a few days, breathing in watery gasps and coughing. When Corlissa goes to wipe Sofia's forehead with a cool cloth, she finds her flushed, a faint smudge of dried sweat across her temples. She's heavy-eyed and weak, like a baby that has yet to open its eyes rooting for the nipple. Corlissa feels protective, and if she puts a name on it, she might call it love. Of course she loves her daughter. She swipes water from the cleaned plate. Of course.

The dishes go into the rack. The sun will dry them quickly. She wipes the counter down with a rag. She hangs it over the faucet. The kitchen is warming fast, so she closes the thin yellow curtains against the glare. She sits down at the table. She turns her hands—backs freckled and blue-veined, nails clipped to small crescents of white, each knuckle deeply lined, and wrinkles, small and faint, running up each finger. The pads of her fingers are still pruned from the washing. She rests her elbow on the table, her head on her palm, and sighs. She wonders what her sisters are doing, or if her mother is still alive. Corlissa's letters to her mother had gone unanswered; after a few years, she stopped trying. The last time she saw her mother was the day Corlissa and Howar announced their intent to marry. Howar had stood in the doorway, reluctant to enter as her mother clanged pots to celebrate her daughter's marriage to a Chinaman. Emily, the last child still at home, leaned against the wall, watching silently until she turned and left the room. Corlissa and Howar boarded the train to Nevada that afternoon.

Everything feels so heavy—Howar's absence, Sofia's sleeping breath, the quiet of the women who move with whisper feet. She feels a blush rising up her face. She fans herself. She has to get out of the house.

In the daytime, the flour mill rattles with business, backs are bent in the gardens, and the pigs slop around happily in the mud, slaughter held off for hours. Bees are drunk among the fennel and goldenrod as she passes through on her way to the tree. She supposes if she were a child she'd have a nickname for the tree, and it would hold delicious surprises, the possibility of fairy pretending or mock battles. Instead, she can see only the strength in the limbs, the bark so tough that it wouldn't bear the friction mark of a rope. She kicks her toe at the roots, upturns the dust, exposing insects and dead grass. A discarded soda bottle lies in the tall weeds; a cork stopper in the shadow of a root. There are candy wrappers and a decaying apple core.

She glances around to see if anyone is coming before tying

her skirt into a knot between her legs and grabbing on to some low branches. She braces her feet against the trunk and pulls herself up. She stands in the first fork and decides to go higher. At the very top, the limbs become thin and tangled in each other, but there are still a good few feet to climb until then. She laughs; she has not climbed a tree since she was a child. She wonders if she noticed then the way the bark eats into the skin and the branches give under the body.

When she has gone as high as she can go, she rests on a limb and lets her legs dangle. There are small scratches on her skin. Her hands are sticky. It feels cooler in the dark web of sticks and leaves. She wipes her forehead sweat on her dress and laughs a little more. She could watch people pass by, listen in on conversations. She twists around to see if there is a view through the branches. She can see a corner of the slough, a spot of star-shiny water, sunlit. Trees and vines cover the rest.

Leaves and twigs break below. She tightens her hands to steady herself. The two women pass beneath. Voices clear as peals. Sai Fung leads with small energetic steps and turns her head back toward So Wai every few words. In Corlissa's child-hood game, she would be a spy, and elusive truths would be revealed in this moment. She holds her breath. Critical words spoken just as the three come into alignment like mysti-cal planets. But the talk is plain. Sai Fung stops to poke at a flower, sniff a little, and brush her finger over the pollen.

So hot. Doesn't it drive people to the water? What we need is rain.

A flood.

Anything. Anything wet. So Wai turns her head and meets Corlissa's eyes through the patchwork of leaves. Corlissa catches her breath. The light shifts, the leaves move, Corlissa exhales. The women walk away.

And then they are over the hump of the hill. Dark figures disappearing beneath a horizon of land. She sees them again a few yards off, walking toward the water. They follow the edge on a soft mud trail and dissolve into a thicket around a bend. Corlissa turns to an ant that crawls across her knee. She pinches it up and drops it to the ground. The childish pleasure of tree climbing seems silly now.

SHE HAS BRUSHES to flurry the dust from the furniture cushions, dusters to sweep across wood surfaces, long-handled bristles for the toilet, sponges for the sink. They have been chosen from the open suitcase of a traveling salesman, or checked off in a catalog order form, sent away for with money tucked in the licked-closed envelope. She has rubber gloves to protect her hands and keep them silky smooth, an apron to tie around her waist. There are a variety of cleaners and soaps—powders, liquids, bars—in tins and cardboard. On their labels there are smiling children, mustachioed men, women in aprons. She has specially treated rags that leave a gloss across the grain of her wood floors.

She drags a cloth across drops of water. The water forms a

trail; she wipes as she follows. The water puddles at the base of the sofa. She mops this up. She glances up, listening for a creak from Sofia's room, some indication that Sofia has been up and about. There is nothing. She peels off her glove and presses into the sofa cushion. It is damp, with the water-dark imprint left by a sitting person.

She's been twice more to inquire about work at Jack Yang's restaurant. And each time he has sidestepped her with claims of too many workers, not enough money. Though many are eager to help by claiming newcomers as a long-lost sister, an actually dead brother, finding tangibles such as housing and money is more difficult. The women's presence is the feeling of walking into a room where the sofa has shifted a foot to the left. The room is still familiar, but one bumps a knee or hip for a week before a new path is learned. Turn one way toward new open space, another way for a bruise. She feels sympathy, but also longs to walk into a room without the fright of coming upon the two women sitting in the dark, without the labor of having to sweep their salt dust from the church, and without the unsettled curiosity of wiping down wet furniture.

THERE'S A LETTER today, the Japanese postmaster says. He reaches into the cubby marked with the Lees' address and brings down a thin envelope with a local postmark. Scrawl like spider legs. Corlissa has nothing to post. The letter is taken with a trepidation that slows to a dawdling through town. The glare of sunlight turns the streets gaudy: the tufts of animal hair caught on a knot of fence, the raw exposed skin on gurgling chickens, dirt clinging to the drying paint on a house. The world matches the ugliness of her impending task. Inside the letter, she already knows, is the news that So Wai's husband cannot be found, or has passed away. When she opens her mouth to tell her, she will watch her breath exhale away a whole world.

In another church, her footsteps would echo. In this modest single room, her entrance is flat and solid. She steps over grains of white salt to the very front and takes a seat. The wooden Christ hangs His head before her. Mournful lines have been etched around His drooping mouth. His belly button is a divot scooped from below, leaving a tiny flap of wooden skin over the top. Even His kneecaps have been carved with care. He is shiny, as if wailing women have stroked the wood with pleading hands. Corlissa has her own plea—that her words will not devastate.

She turns her head at shuffling through the door. The women are surprised to see her. Her weak smile is too revealing.

I found berries, Sai Fung says. In her outstretched palm, bruised blackberries and pink stains. Little seeds speckle her teeth.

We can make a pie, Corlissa says. Then to So Wai: A letter for you came. I think it's in English.

So Wai blinks at the Christ. Read it, please.

Corlissa nicks the corner, under the flap, with her fingernail and peels the top of the envelope. When the tear is a bit wider, she rips it open in jagged intervals. She wishes Howar were here. The letter is addressed to him; it would be his responsibility.

Dear Sir,

Regarding Yee Wei-fan; he arrived in May of 1923 in San Francisco and was employed, as of November 1927, at the Smith farm near Stockton. On November 22 of last year, Mr. Yee succumbed to tuberculosis and was buried in the Chinamen's cemetery. We are very sorry to inform you of this news.

So Wai does not move. Corlissa refolds the letter and puts it back in the envelope.

Completely futile, So Wai says. Sai Fung curls her fingers around the berries. Juice bleeds into her knuckles. She touches So Wai's shoulder. Corlissa tenses. She waits for panicked breath, a collapse to the ground, a warbling mourner's scream.

He's in a better place, she says. Don't feel ashamed to cry, Corlissa urges.

So Wai takes the letter and presses it between her palms. Not knowing was worse than this.

Sai Fung sets the berries on a seat and clasps So Wai's hands between her own.

Corlissa rolls the berries into her hand, rubs her finger over a spot. She's embarrassed to watch the grief and comforting.

She shrugs past them. Just a couple of bites, not enough for a pie. Still warm from the vine. If she lost Howar, she'd drown herself.

CORLISSA HATES THE feeling of walking back home in the heat. The town is quiet, most people drawing into their homes for dinner, a few small children racing tricycles around a neighbor's truck. The dogs are too tired to rise and merely follow the action with their eyes.

This is the feeling of death.

The thought startles Corlissa and gives her goose bumps. She opens the front door and steps into the living room. The curtains are drawn and the windows are closed. She's filled with such sadness, such a hunger for sunshine and open windows. The air feels warm and sad and Corlissa's sure that it comes from outside herself. For a moment, she hears So Wai's scream, like a fox being torn apart by hounds.

Corlissa drops the berries on Howar's desk, claws her way out of the muffled room, and climbs the stairs. The clinging sadness has not left her, even beyond the reach of the living room. Corlissa lies down on the bed to cry.

34

RICHARD HEARS THE kitchen floor squeak. She's up already, in the dawn light. He stretches his arms and legs across the bed, reveling in the space. He hears the clang of a pot, the whisper of water. He runs the back of his hand across his nose. A trail of moisture shines on his skin. He wipes his nose again, with the sheet.

He will not work today. They'd sent him home from the Lucky Fortune just a few days ago, after he'd gone upstairs to the guard's quarters and fallen asleep on the thin mattress. He had told them he was going upstairs to check up on things, but the heat in the little room had made him sleepy. He had writhed on the sheets, searching for cool spots. He shifted each time his body warmed the sheets and looked for another cool, untouched part of the bed. Finally, he'd fallen into a nap, breathing mustiness and lulled by the blurred roar below. When he stumbled downstairs, they tactfully ignored the redness in his eyes, the wetness that lined his nostrils, and suggested that he go home.

A breeze whistles in around the window border. Richard

pulls the top sheet over his shoulder. More sounds from the kitchen—scraping, a tinkle of light glass, shuffling. Ming Wai has insomnia. He knows she often lies awake long after he has drifted into sleep. She gets up before him and rackets around the apartment as if she wants to be sure her presence is noticed. On occasion, he has opened his eyes and found her watching him. She sits in the small chair in the corner. When he asks what she is doing, she quickly faces the floor and says she has lost something. What? he asks. She doesn't answer.

But she has not done that in a while. Richard reaches out and pulls the curtain aside. He doesn't know what he expects to find; the view is the same every day—the brown wall of the building next door. Stained mattress propped on the landing. Gray sky beyond the lines of the roof. She's singing now. He would shout for her to be quiet, but it is his favorite lullaby— a song his mother used to sing to him about a baby kidnapped by spirits to be raised in the mountains. The baby came down the mountain as a man to search for his old mother. He found the end of a tapestry and followed miles of brilliant woolen color to her hut. Ten feet woven for every day of his absence. It flowed through the door, across the garden, around the house, along the river, and to the mountain. At the doorway of the hut, the man looked in on his mother. She wove with squinting eyes, hand shaking at the loom.

His mouth feels sticky, his lips coated with film. He runs two fingers over his teeth and gums. He wipes his mouth on the sheet again. He should get up. The blurriness of his unremembered dreams is gone; the traces of sleep have been stretched out of his body. He hasn't left the apartment since he came home from the Lucky Fortune. He sits up and opens the window. The air is cold and fresh.

He moans a little as he pulls himself from bed. Through the doorway, across the living room, and into the kitchen. Vegetable crates and crumpled newspaper surround Ming Wai. She stands on a chair, reaching her small arms into the cabinet. She pulls down glasses, steps carefully from the chair with a gasp, and sets them next to the other dishes hidden in paper.

What are you doing?

She pours some hot water into a mug. Drink some. Sit down.

What are you doing? She's flushed from the work and her hair is falling loose from its braid.

I don't want these things anymore. Look, I bought these instead. She pries open a box and takes out a blue dish from curls of packing straw.

The money?

This place isn't so big. I found where you keep it. They delivered these this morning. Here, new linens. And this music box. She cranks the key. A little girl and boy, holding hands, spin around to the music.

But these are my things.

If he wasn't so weak, he'd pack them up again, demand that she return them, perhaps break one to prove his outrage.

She sits on the floor and wraps the glasses in newspaper. Richard sits at the table and sips the water. But these are my things, he says again.

After you left, Siu Dai's wife made all the decisions.

Siu Dai's wife?

Yes. She unfolds a napkin. Pretty?

Sure, sure. Why didn't you write to me?

And run to you like a big brother? How could anyone respect me then? I still don't understand why you have an icebox and they have an electric one. America is funny.

Tell me more.

She wipes down her new plates and carefully stacks them.

I have nothing to say.

Where did you sleep? Did you have a servant?

Sometimes with the children, mostly in your old room. A servant, yes.

I worked in the pear orchard, he says. His life had been harder, he wants her to know. She would like him to feel guilty for leaving her to the mercy of his brother and his wife, but his life had been harder.

I slept in a room full of men, some of them had no beds, and we worked sunup to sundown, in weather hotter than this. Weather so hot, every breath was a curse. They say that a man died and went to hell, then had the opportunity to be reborn in Sacramento. Well, he pleaded to be sent back to hell, because Sacramento was too damn hot. Every day in that weather.

You were uncomfortable. She sets the music box on the

counter and turns the key. A tinny, unrecognizable song whimpers out.

Tired to the bone. Hot. Sunburnt. Hungry sometimes too.

All easily remedied, she says. Hungry? Eat. Hot? Step into the shade. Tired? Go to sleep. You came by choice.

I came for us. An old line, repeated before he left, then in his letters.

I lost a husband. I lost face. How do you remedy that, Fong Man Gum? She opens the icebox. The shelves are bare and wiped down.

35

THE POSTMASTER RUNS a little bank out of a safe behind the counter. Someone stealthy has click-clicked the lock open and removed a thousand dollars. Only the postmaster has the combination. It would have taken a careful ear and steady, light fingers to sense the tiny catches where the magic numbers are revealed. A bit of dirt on the floor in front of the safe where the thief crouched, but no shoe print. The postmaster is not a sleuth, but he has a hunch. It is just past dawn; he may be able to retrieve the money.

The sack lies on the preacher's stoop, too big for its contents, sagging from empty space. The postmaster thrusts his hand inside, finds the neatly banded stacks of money. The thief is stupid too—he's attached a note with his name. His wealth is not just boasting and here's the proof. No one is stirring yet. The postmaster's heart begins to pound. Is it unethical what he does? He tears the note from the twine. With the pencil that is perpetually tucked behind his ear and a slip of paper from his breast pocket, he scribbles something new. His name. His wealth is not just boasting and here's the proof.

36

POPPY LOOKS ACROSS the street and sees something she has never seen before. Women, dressed up and laughing, walk into the Lucky Fortune. She pushes up the window and leans out. Yes, women, dressed up like the dreams of Hollywood in spangles and feathers. They're having a party and she has not been invited.

Even children arrive, holding their mothers' hands. She sniffs. There are the delicate scents of cakes and soda pop and perfume and shaving cream. The smell of freshly brushed teeth. Something good and wholesome is happening in the gambling hall.

TODAY IS THE day that the Weaving Maiden and the Ox Herd join across a river of stars. After the two fell in love and neglected their jobs—spiders overtook the loom and the oxen roamed hungry—angry gods separated them and forbade them to meet, save for on this one night, when Vega and Altair cross the Milky Way. It is a day for reunited lovers.

In the doorway of the Lucky Fortune, Richard greets

guests. It's a monumental day in the gambling hall's history—
the first time women have been allowed to enter. The party cel-
ebrates Richard's return to work, Ming Wai's arrival, and the
Festival of the Weaving Maiden. All the respectable families
in town have been invited. Richard is tired of dusty floors and
wet spittoons. He has covered the gaming tables with pretty
cloths, laid out flowers and cookies, even bottles of wine.

He's weaker than ever. He has had to hammer out new
notches in his belt and his shirt hangs loose in an unbecom-
ing style. The tenderness in his feet gives him ginger steps.
But his heart feels stronger. He had left China not quite in
love with his wife. He has grown older here going about his life
without her. But he has felt her here and not here, and he knows
what choice he would make, over and over. She stands across
the room talking to the other boat-women. The three of them
stand under a lantern, their faces tight with interest. Ming Wai
looks vibrant. Her hair is glossy and her eyes shine back every
light in the room. Over there is the preacher, his whitewife,
and their daughter; there, the owner of the haberdashery up
the street; there, the butcher; and so forth. A few laborers have
come as well, friends of Richard's, those on a midweek break or
out of work. As always, the men outnumber the women.

THE PREACHER WOULD like to expand the church and its
role in town. With his hands, he indicates the current layout of the
north end of Second Street. His pinched thumb and fingers—a

hand curving into a teardrop—bounce from here to there to represent buildings. The polish of a palm on an imaginary surface draws an invisible street. He pushes up his glasses. One listener falters, turns and fiddles with lighting a cigar. The preacher's pause is a brief hiccup before he sweeps back into his gesturing and deep-night plans. The man with the cigar turns away to take some cookies. He eats as he watches the preacher talk. Crumbs fall on his shirt. He fans them away with his free hand. Hunger relieved, he renews his gaze on this newcomer who takes Bible learning as civic intelligence, who funnels a planner's dreams and a founder's pride into plans discussed under the Coleman lanterns of a minor gambling hall in a small Delta town.

THE AUBURN-HAIRED GIRL stands against a table, sipping at a small cup of coffee. The other teenagers stand near a different table, giggling over glasses of soda. She watches them with a blank expression. She takes another sip and winces. She looks to see if anyone is watching. She scratches her nose. She looks again at the other girls. With her free hand, she tugs at her dress, slides an untied ribbon through her fingers again and again. When one of the girls glances over, relief breaks over her face. She smiles.

THE WHITEWOMAN IS at the edge of a circle of women. She nods with every emphatic word spoken by the others.

When the attention turns to her, her posture does not falter, though she reddens a little beneath her freckles. She speaks, and the others lean forward. Then they nod, and the conversation returns to the squat woman with the wild gestures. The whitewoman stands very still, her hands clasped before her, a crumpled napkin held between them.

THREE WOMEN HUDDLE near a wall. They are blue-hazed, lighting up the corner. The youngest chatters for a bit, then falls silent, and no one answers, not the long-absent wife or the new widow. The one in mourning steps away and backs to the wall. The other two join her. They all have long black hair twisted into buns and eyes that flash and burn with dead light.

RICHARD HOLDS HIS hand up for attention and says in English, Excuse me, excuse me. The hush travels unevenly around the room, silence emerging from pockets of people until the Lucky Fortune goes quiet.

He coughs. Thank you for coming. I hope all ladies and gentlemen will pause for a moment and enjoy a song. My wife and her friends arrived nearly two months ago. They would like to play something to express their thanks for your hospitality.

The women begin as a chorus, together like the shudder of goose wings. Two voices fall away. So Wai sings alone. Her voice rises and collapses, whimpers and soars. The listeners who can't tease out the words think of the last embers of a campfire doused with sand, or an old woman in the throes of death calling for her mother. The hairs on Richard's arm rise.

Those who came as couples seek each other's hands for the comfort of skin. The women think of their husbands, the men they loved before their husbands, and the girlhood friends they'd loved before the men. The men think of dreams discarded, the wives left behind, or the wives still to be found. And the children try to wrap their minds around a future not yet imagined.

Nothing flickers, not an eye nor a flame.

There is the girl across the street. Sofia imagines her leaning over her sill, straining for this song like a girl longing for the moon. And the paper moon, flimsy and faking the real deal, yearns right back for her. Sofia can't think her way to the future promised by the song when the present, twenty steps away, is held at bay.

Corlissa finds herself waist-deep in the accumulation of the years. Her love building color like layers of paint. Devotion another plane intersecting with time and space. She looks across the room and catches Richard's eye. He quickly looks away.

Song, like scent, is a wrist-flick to the past. Richard is there and there and there. He doesn't just think of Ming Wai, but of the family he has not seen for a decade. In every minute, in the million decisions he has made to come from there to here, a decade has passed. On his family's side too, a million decisions, a divergence wider than this ocean. The word that Ming Wai has not yet dared to whisper: abandonment.

The song ends. Women gather their coats and their children. The men put on their hats. No one can bring themselves to utter a word of good night or thanks and they trudge silently to their homes. The laborers forget the wine and the brothels and disperse to the fields, each making love with a fist. The husbands and wives shut their doors behind themselves. Their hearts skip with the click of the latch.

POPPY STEPS THROUGH the open door of the Lucky Fortune. The whole place is deserted but the lanterns burn brightly. Food lies half eaten on the tables, cups half empty. She walks through, touching every warm seat, every fingerprinted glass. She dips her finger into the punch bowl and licks it. She presses cake crumbs to her tongue. She hears the song still resonating. It hides under tables, edges itself into corners, and waits. When she touches the wall, she feels the warmth of Richard's hand on her pregnant stomach. She feels the ghost of a never-been baby turn inside her. She steps backward to the front of the Lucky Fortune and quietly closes the door.

37

The Never-Been Baby (1927)

THOUGH THE DOCTOR had said Poppy See would never have children, every night for a month she had dreamt of babies. A baby arriving. But there was never the moment of its arrival—one moment it was not there; then, simply, it was. A shock of black hair, rolls of biscuity fat, and when it turned its eyes to her, the startle of blue eyes. All babies have blue eyes when they're born, she told herself. Some nights, she woke from these dreams when it was still dark, stretched her hand for the lamp, and clicked it on. The room came up pink. She stared at the red and gold fleur-de-lis wallpaper for a few moments, until Richard muttered, What is it?

Another baby dream.

If you stop thinking of babies, you'll stop dreaming of them. Shut off the light. Richard pressed his face into the pillow.

Poppy clicked the lamp off and her hand drifted to her stomach. She rubbed and massaged, feeling for a swell, or the faintness of a heartbeat. All she felt was her pulse and the movement of her own breath.

WHEN THE TIME was right, she checked for blood. Any cramp or unsettling of her stomach sent her to the bathroom. But there was only clean cotton. In the mornings, she imagined nausea. She stirred at her rice porridge, slowly, until George asked, Are you sick? She shook her head, forced a spoonful of the watery gruel into her mouth, and swallowed. She coughed, but the food stayed down. George watched her and scratched at a tattoo. Its ink had bled, blurring the lines of a daggered heart.

A baby would be an excuse to leave. In the afternoons, when the girls lounged in the parlor waiting for customers, Poppy watched them in a kind of self-satisfied wonder. Sixteen years ago, she never would have imagined that she would have white-girls working for her. It was a power reversal that gave her a flutter of giddiness. However, it was a giddiness she would trade for the smell of talcum and sleepy-eyed milk drunkenness.

That the baby would be Richard's child increased the joy. Poppy was settled by the fact that his wife was far away and he had not seen her in nine years. The town had a few such men: split and living two lives—one in China, through paper, with a wife remembered only through a photograph, and one in America with flesh and blood. Richard showed no interest in returning, and it seemed unlikely that his wife could come over to America, despite the merchant status that Richard had been angling to establish. Poppy might never be his wife, but the role of concubine, of lover, was not distasteful to her.

. . .

SHE WAS LOSING the baby. In the dark, her hands went to her stomach, then between her legs as if to hold it in. She had just woken from a dream of a dead baby slipping down a bloody well. It was a girl, she saw. As the dark shapes in the room assumed definition to her adjusting eyes, she told herself that she would want a girl as much as a boy. She muttered this to the baby, cooing, urging it to stay. Richard hushed her, grumbled a bit, and threw his arm across her stomach.

Don't, she whispered in the dark. Her voice was so meek, she could barely hear herself. Don't, she said.

But he was sleeping, and his arm remained.

SHE HAD HEADACHES, because she refused to drink anymore. She tried to mold herself to her fantasy of motherhood: an ascetic woman clothed in somber black. The thimbleful of liquor, gulped surreptitiously in the morning, or in the afternoon (to settle her—the doctor recommended it), no longer marked the hours of her day. Without the drink, there was dizziness, rising anxiety. She felt the pressure in her blood. She wrapped the bottle of scotch in towels, dragged a chair to the closet, and stuffed the bottle to the very back of the top shelf.

The girls began to turn away when she entered the room. They were suddenly taken with the tasks of magazine reading or darning. Or staring at their hands. They wouldn't cross her path, and this apprehension made her even more irritated. She snapped at them, and though they were fighters, unafraid of throwing a punch in a saloon or insulting a customer, they bit their lips and took her words. When she turned, focused on the pounding blood at the center of her stomach, she heard a whisper of conversation that grew the farther away she walked.

WORK WOULD MAKE her stronger. No longer concerned only with bookkeeping, she washed laundry and dishes, and cooked. She was wringing water from a shirt when there was a knock at the back door. She shook out the shirt, laid it on the tile countertop, and went to answer.

A well-dressed whitegirl in a beautiful camel-hair coat stood before her. The girl's blond hair had grown scraggly, and her face was free of makeup. Despite the ragged edges, she was young and pretty. Baby-faced, with loose good looks that fell just short of vulgar. She was pregnant.

I need some help, she said. Her arms hugged her stomach and her smile failed.

I'm not a midwife, Poppy said. She raised her eyes for a moment from the seductive swell of the girl's belly.

Can I just sit, ma'am? The girl frowned, as if pain lurked just beneath her calm words.

Poppy let her in and as she shut the door behind her, she saw the spots of blood bright on the girl's dress.

How far along are you?

Just seven months, the girl said. She sat on the sofa and groaned.

What's your name?

Chloe, ma'am. Again, a groan. Yours?

Madam See. I think you better come to the kitchen.

The girl walked with her legs awkwardly apart, whimpering the whole way.

In the kitchen, Poppy placed a pan on the floor and told the girl to squat over it. She put a pot of water on the stove. She hollered for George.

Chloe steadied herself by gripping two chairs. Her dress pulled up over her knees, the lower half of her belly exposed. Small drops of blood spattered into the pan.

Did someone hit you? Did you fall? Poppy asked. She yelled for George again.

No, ma'am. I was just on the ferry from SF and I started hurting. Chloe breathed sharply.

George walked into the room with Richard.

What's this? Richard asked. He was suited and still wore his hat; he had come over from the Lucky Fortune for a break.

A baby, Poppy said. She bit down her smile. A baby, a baby had just arrived at her back door.

Chloe closed her eyes and scrunched her face. She moaned. In the reflection of the bottom of the pan, Poppy saw a glimmer of scalp swirled with dark hair.

It's coming, she said. Don't worry, girl, it's coming. I see the head.

George remained stoic. Watch the water, Poppy said. Richard slipped off his jacket and crouched beside the two women.

Chloe grunted and the waste and blood that streamed from her body obscured Poppy's view in the pan.

Richard said, You can squeeze my hand. Poppy looked up at his words. She saw him slip his hand into Chloe's and the softness in his eyes. She'd never seen his face so concerned, nor heard his voice so slack in soothing. He whispered to Chloe. Poppy couldn't hear his words. They were lost to the panting and the moaning, but it was the tone of the hush, the rhythm of the comfort that mattered. The baby's head emerged. Poppy put her hands underneath to catch its body.

Chloe let out an abridged yell. She rocked a little as she pushed. Pull it out! she yelled. Pull it out! The neck and shoulders slipped free and the rest of the baby slid slippery-quick into Poppy's hand. The umbilical cord was wrapped around its neck.

George, a knife! Quickly, a knife! Poppy yelled. She tried to wedge her fingers beneath the thick ropes, to loosen them. George handed her a knife and she carefully cut the cord. Blood dribbled out, and still the baby didn't breathe.

It's dead, Chloe said. She began to cry and collapsed onto the floor, onto her dress, seeming not to care if it became matted with blood. Richard stroked her hair.

Poppy massaged the baby girl's broken neck, her tiny chest. She was half the size of a full-term baby and in the quiet of the moment, Poppy noticed the gray skin. Each finger, each piece, perfectly formed, but as limp and discolored as a doll's. She glanced at Richard; his attention was still on Chloe.

Do you want to see it? she asked.

Chloe sobbed and shook her head.

Do you want to know what sex it is? Poppy still held the baby as if it were alive, sleeping soundly in cradled arms, staining Poppy's sleeves with blood.

Chloe shook her head again.

I'm going to take it away now, Poppy said. Chloe was still crying and she wouldn't open her eyes. She nodded.

Poppy wrapped it in a dish towel, bundled it up, covering even its face. She left the brothel and crossed the street, walked down an alley, past Second Street, past all the houses and gardens to the incinerator. The iron door opened with a squeal and the heat was instantly warming.

She uncovered the baby's face and touched the tiny nose, the little pout and closed lids. She cried a little, for it and for herself. She folded the cloth back down. She put her ear to its chest to be sure there was not a small, faint beat. The body was already losing the warmth of Chloe's body. Poppy closed her eyes for a moment, then tossed the baby into the fire.

38

SINCE THE PARTY on Tuesday, Richard's days have taken on a steady rhythm. He dreams of Ming Wai. They go about banal tasks—cooking, sewing, reading, walking. She never leaves him. She sits on the edge of the tub when he is on the toilet. She touches the nape of his neck when he brushes his teeth. Asleep, she is there. Awake, she is there.

When he can manage it, she feeds him ham and boiled chicken and softened crackers. After a few bites, he falls asleep again and the food goes sour in his mouth. Between the dreaming and the eating, they make love. The sadness of Tuesday's song still lingers, drawing up curiosity about what luck or misfortune brought Ming Wai here, and confusion at her elusiveness. When wisps of the song drift through his head, he feels like he's crouched in the woods without the will to scream, watching a retreating trail of lanterns bob over hills and disappear into valleys.

Maybe this is what weakens him: Ming Wai, who asks for more and more and more of him.

She sits, curled at the end of the bed, the curtain brushed

aside with her hand. He looks at the gnarled breaks in her feet. She turns away from the window.

He smiles, then licks at the dry bits of skin on his lips. He tastes blood.

What are you watching? he asks.

It's going to rain, she says.

Are there clouds?

Not yet.

Then how do you know?

My feet ache.

He nods. Could I have some water?

Next to the bed. She looks back out the window.

Richard feels around for the glass. He watches her over the rim as he drinks. She looks lovely in the sunlight. She's gained weight. Her cheeks are full and rosy. Her skin is not so icy.

Fong Man Gum, she says. Do you?

Fong Man Gum? he thinks. That's me. He had forgotten for a moment.

Do you remember the weather on our wedding day?

He closes his eyes and sees sunshine—a bright ball of white shining on red dirt. It was summer, he says.

And it rained. And I cried because my feet hurt so badly.

It rained? Of course—it was the rainy season, Richard thinks. He licks at his dry lips and hums his agreement.

You don't remember?

I forgot. He opens his eyes. She lets the curtain fall back, but she still glows like sunlight. He doesn't know if he is dreaming or awake. He wiggles his toes and scratches some wax from his ear. Even movement and detritus can't convince him.

She leaves the bed, leaves the room. He hears her move through the apartment. In a building so precariously built, each of her footsteps resonates in the shuddering legs of the bed. He turns on his side and presses his face into the pillow. The wedding party had trampled through mud, taking care not to splatter her trousseau when they carried it across the village into his home. And there was the beating of rain on the roof when he undressed her.

Are you going out? he calls.

She walks to the doorway and looks in on him as she combs her hair. She smiles. No, Fong Man Gum, the whole town is closed.

Is it a holiday? Richard tries to remember what day it is— the month, the date.

She smiles and shrugs. She struggles the comb through a tangle and, concentrating on the task, walks away from the room again.

It's true—Richard cannot recall his sleep being marred by the thumping of the bok-bok man calling out the time. He hasn't heard the pigs screaming, or even an engine rumble over Main Street. He listens for people and hears only the ragged whistle of his breathing. He pulls his knees to his chest and puts the pillow over his head. He falls back asleep in the muffled darkness.

39

CHLOE WALKS IN circles around the empty beds in the hot attic of late afternoon. Madam See says that this happens sometimes—villages fall into a stupor, people make love for days, food is forgotten, spiders spin webs across storefronts, and the animals rut and cry to be fed. It has been nearly a week since any men have crossed the threshold of the brothel, and many of the girls have gone home or to the city to wait for the plague to pass. The sound of crickets has overtaken the evenings—it seems that they have also bred, multiplied their numbers so that every ceiling crack and porch plank vibrates with their singing.

Chloe sits on Lisel's bed. She tries to fit herself into the imprint worn into the mattress. But Lisel is bigger, sleeps awkwardly to ease her crippled arm, and Chloe cannot fit. She stands up and the relieved springs sigh. She lies on Beatrice's bed. Beatrice is a side sleeper, and she has spent so many nights with her beau in Walnut Grove that the springs have righted themselves and there is only the faintest shadow of her presence. Her pillow smells of hair cream.

Chloe misses Sofia. She fell down inside when they parted in the store, and it was a different sort of falling down from what happened with Alfred. It was the kind of falling down where everything falls into little pieces. But she hadn't cried. Instead, she thought of New York, of Ruby the jazz singer. Her clear strong voice and the world she moved through—smoke-screened, cigar-scented, women in red dresses. Just thinking of the songs made Chloe stronger, and she'd gone upstairs and counted up her savings. It was nearly enough to leave, and she planned for September. She would hitch a ride to Sacramento. There were places that rented to working girls—real, legitimate places—and she had enough for a month's rent at least.

Just as Alfred had taught her—it was all about remaking oneself. You could be just a girl from the Central Valley, then turn into a New York moll. From that, an unmarried pregnant girl wandering San Francisco, then, before you could blink a tear, you were a whore, back in the Central Valley. And nobody could trace you through all those different girls, because they knew only what they could see.

The light coming through the diamond window shifts and the room turns from sun-shafted to gray. Chloe rises from Beatrice's bed and goes to the window. Clouds cover the sun and start filling the sky. Chloe presses her hand against the glass; the heat is fading fast. Maybe rain is what the town needs. Maybe rain will cool the passions, drive the people from their beds and back to work.

Chloe walks back to her bed. A motley pile of things she plans to take litters the top. She scoots to her knees and sweeps her hand through the darkness beneath the bed for anything she might have forgotten.

40

EIGHT DAYS AFTER the town fell into the lull of lovemaking, and the crickets poured out of the fields and overtook the road, Poppy puts out offerings for Ghost Month. On a table in front of the brothel, she piles up tins of ham, boxes of crackers, a boiled chicken, oranges, bottles of soda. She places lit joss sticks among them and shakes her steepled hands three times. She burns money for the returning dead—a bribery to appease their unhappy souls—and watches as the wind lifts the light ash out of the barrel in a tunnel of smoke and paper flakes that carries the burnt hell notes over the rooftops of Locke.

Since Sunday, she has heard the rumblings on the other side, the gathering of spirits readying for their once-yearly visit to earth. This morning, as she collected her food offerings, she heard the scream of the hinges as the door to the underworld opened. The Festival of the Hungry Ghost is an old holiday, old already when her grandmother put out offerings on this same lunar day, old already when her grandmother's grandmother burned incense for ancient ghosts. It is past the point of useful belief and ritual. Perhaps only to Poppy, above all others who put out their gifts and mutter their chants, does it signify anything. Every year, all the buildings crowd with ghosts, so packed she has to suck in her breath to pass through. The girls of the brothel do not seem to notice, and Poppy does not bother to explain. The rumbling this year, however, feels different. The source, Poppy thinks, is the three ice-blue women. From the hush-hushes in town, and the gasps of the men who file into the brothel, she knows that the women's hands are cold, that they cast their own faint light (luminous, one man said), and their utterances are detached and hollow. She whispers a few words of protection for Richard, throws a look at the gathering clouds, and goes back inside.

41

ON THE FIRST night of Ghost Month, the rain begins.

Warm rain, clapping thunder, even lightning. The rain thunders against the metal roofs, muddies the roads, soaks into the roots of the willows and sycamores on Main Street. The rain washes the gasoline stains from the dirt around the pump and the blood from the yard of the slaughterhouse.

It's the kind of rain that keeps people in. The men stay in the bunkhouses, sitting on crates, their hands full of cards, making their fun with bootleg and cigarettes. The inside clatter rises up to beat the outside clatter. In bedrooms around town, men and women break, exhausted, from their week-long embrace, glance down at their emaciated bodies, dress quickly, and hurry to the kitchen for food. The sound of the rain makes them ache for water.

THE RAIN DRAWS Corlissa from her room. She has been in here without food or real sleep. It takes her a moment to remember this fact, and the memory must rise up through all her immediate senses—the heaviness in her chest, the soreness in her throat, and her constant thirst. Howar sleeps next to her. His glasses are on the floor. She tiptoes out of bed and opens the door.

She has forgotten Sofia. Who has fed her, cared for her this whole week? It panics her to realize she has forgotten her daughter. She glides down the hall, led from plank to plank by the shattered illumination of lightning. Sofia's door is ajar. Inside, hushed talking like a murmur into a neck. Sofia has the blankets pulled to her chin. She listens sleepily to a story, lulled by words she can't understand. Sai Fung sits at the end of the bed; So Wai, in a chair at the bedside. In the space of moments, So Wai's face darkens to soft shadows, then explodes into the wide, light planes of her cheeks and the blue glaze of her eyes. She tells a story. Corlissa leans into the doorway to listen:

As the most talented and beautiful singing girl, Young Jade was selective. Only men with the highest honors or positions could hope to be rewarded with a look or a dance. One day, a high dignitary crossed her province. A feast was given. In the midst of the dancing, singing, eating, the dignitary clapped his hands and demanded to be shown Young Jade. Out she came, with peony cheeks and glossy sparrow hair. The dignitary declared that she was the most beautiful singing girl in the east and west, but in this small province, no one would ever know this. As she sang, he scribbled out some couplets to her, promising to make her name widely known. Her reputation grew, but so did her melancholy. On every occasion, she sought solitude. When asked why, she sighed, This life and I are not well suited.

A bit more prying revealed this: She was tired of the ointments and powders, of being dolled up like a whore. She despised superficial conversation, and the lewdness she was forced to endure. All she wanted, she said, was to be somebody's wife.

Not long after this declaration, she crossed paths with a handsome young man from the east. From that afternoon on, they were inseparable. The young man hid himself in her chamber every night. Young Jade's heart had never been so light. But her happiness drew suspicion. Her patron became jealous and threatened to denounce the young man to the authorities. The young man had too much to lose, so he stopped visiting Young Jade.

One afternoon, their boats crossed on the lake. With dainty steps, Young Jade passed into his boat for a few stolen moments of conversation. She told him to disregard her dancing partner's jealousy. When the young man refused, Young Jade revealed a secret. In her heart, she believed that her bones would be buried with his ancestors. No matter the distance or obstacles, their love would succeed. In order to prove her devotion, she unpinned her hair. It thudded to the floor of the boat. Her hair was her gold, she said, but for him, she would cut it. He nearly cried with joy as her knife swept through her hair. But the sacrifice only heightened the pain he felt at their parting. Within days, he fell ill.

Young Jade sent her friends to look after him, and after some time, he recovered. His parents demanded he return home. On the eve of his departure, he met Young Jade in a country tavern for one last time. She declared that their match was fated, and so she would wait for him. They passed the night in an inn next to a river. In the morning, they parted.

Despite the young man's promise, he was unable to convince his elderly parents that he should marry the singing girl. He spent his days weeping in front of his mirror. He drank wine to ease his soul, but this only worsened his mood. He even wished for death. One day, a traveler brought a letter from Young Jade. The young man's hands shook as he tore it open, and his eyes caught on the last couplet:

The spring silkworm ceases spinning only at death
The candle's tears cease only when it burns to ash.

He hastily sent a reply, urging Young Jade to maintain her health if there was ever to be hope of their meeting.

One evening, as the sun set, a woman with a veiled face came through the haze of the young man's bedchamber. It was Young Jade. She moved like mist. Incredulous, he reached his hand toward her.

I wasted away with longing, she said. But I will be reborn as the daughter of the baker down the road. If you remember me, you may visit. I won't remember you, but my passion will be the same. Again, she vowed her eternal love, then dissipated like sun-burned fog.

The young man was struck dumb with disbelief. His doubt continued a few days more until a traveler came with the news of Young Jade's death. From his knapsack, the traveler unwrapped nail clippings and a strand of her hair. With her dying breath, she had urged he take these to the young man as a greeting and a farewell.

In the context of the rain, it is a ghost story. The chill that awoke Corlissa shakes her again. In the context of this week, it is a love story, redoubling around, like the silkworm's thread, the faith in fate. She recalls another idiom Howar had taught her. It takes a hundred years of fate to bring two people to a shared boat ride; a thousand years of fate to bring two people to the same pillow. She saves herself from his romantic mumblings: Fate. The excuse that saves us from the terror of our decisions.

CORLISSA SITS ACROSS the kitchen table from Howar like a shy lover. She holds back the impulse to slither her toe up his bare leg and concentrates instead on her sandwich. The contents of the icebox are spread over the table between them—most of it wilted or rotting. The ice tray is dry—the melted ice has already evaporated away.

She pushes through her grogginess and tries to emerge from the dream-thoughts of a half-remembered week. Her hair is matted and speaking is uncertain. She notices the thick dust on the table, on the dishes in the rack, over the cupboard panes, and how hard the chair beneath her is.

I feel like we've just met, Howar says. He has left his glasses upstairs and his bare eyes look drowsy.

Corlissa blinks and when she opens her eyes, she looks at her husband as if she has not seen him in years. The lines draw down around his mouth and there are creases beneath his cheeks. His hair fell out strand by strand; this she didn't notice. She's always seen him as he was when they married. If they passed on the street, after a separation of those sixteen years, would she recognize him with his thinned eyebrows, broken capillaries across his nose? Her skin is soft and loose beneath her wedding ring, her knuckles swollen. She picks up a spoon and looks at her distorted reflection. She looks like a mother. Even in streaked silver she can see the dark moons beneath her eyes. It makes her chest ache, to see herself and her husband, aged around a kitchen table. She runs her fingers over the bones rising in her chest. Rain patters against the window and she wonders exactly how much time has passed. Lightning brightens the sky. The window and everything before it explodes, fast and teasing as a wink.

WATER RISES TO the doorsills and threatens to spill over.

DESPITE THE RAIN, Poppy opens the windows. She needs the air against the stifle of so many spirits in the room. She cools herself on the breeze, then takes a light coat and squeezes down the stairs past the line of ghost-men who clomp up, waiting for brothel services.

One minute from her door to the Men's Center and she is already in disarray, wet-slick and muddy-heeled. She runs her hands along her stockings to wipe the water to the floor. She puts the umbrella in a bucket by the door and rushes to Uncle Happy in the back.

Little Poppy, you shouldn't be out in this weather. He smacks his mouth and smoke pops out in bursts.

Good evening, Uncle Happy. Never mind the rain. I need to talk to you. She sits on the edge of the bench, hesitant about settling against her wet clothing. She wrinkles her nose at the smell of wet boots and spicy smoke.

How long do you think the rain will last? he asks. I have this scar, this one, across my elbow here, that aches. I say three days. This feels like a long spell.

Poppy looks around the room at the ghost-men, who gamble, who crouch on the floor for dominoes and marble games, who drink tea and smoke long pipes. She touches her hand to Uncle Happy's sagging arm to quiet his words and, for a second, feels the trauma of when he received the cut during a fight in a camp, a month after his arrival. All that surging anger, the swell of young-man pride until the knife sang across his skin so clean and sharp. She drops her hand.

Remember my dreams? About the ghosts?

Fong Man Gum's wife, he says.

You should see him, Uncle Happy. He looks awful. She's eating him alive.

It's the fifteenth. First day of Ghost Month.

Exactly. There's something going on. A woman does not arrive out of nowhere like that.

Happy laughs. He drags his nails through the kinky hair of his beard. He says, She's trying to steal his life?

His spirit, his essence.

Ghosts are never good at disguises. What kind is she?

They. There are three of them. And I think they are . . . Poppy pauses and looks through the doorway at the flashes of falling rain. She leans forward to whisper the two words in his ear, then catches herself. She takes a scrap of newspaper from the table next to him and scribbles out the characters. The water off her hand blurs the ink. The words—water ghosts—are too dangerous to be spoken. She shows him the paper as she utters the euphemism: They came from the river.

Maybe he's happy. Maybe he wants to be destroyed. There's a kind of man who will go for that.

Poppy breathes heavily. This answer does not satisfy her. She wants Richard as she has known him—with his languid eyes, his dawn walk in the hall, his snap and impatience at silliness. She leans forward and whispers urgently, What can I do? What do I do? Do I use fire? Do I give them gold?

Happy laughs—a long, shaking laugh that startles Poppy. He takes her hands between his, and she loses her hope before he even speaks: It's all superstition. I stopped burning dead money forty years ago. These dates—they stick in my mind: Ghost Month, Tomb Sweeping Day. I try to forget them, but the memory pops up. Things I used to do. But do I believe them? There are no ghosts. There is no such thing, little Poppy. No ghosts—only our regrets.

AT DAWN, THE rain stops. People stir at the silence. In a half-dreaming space, they nod at the lone drips of water falling off the roof and forget the stopped rain as soon as they fall back asleep. When the town awakes fully, the rain has returned.

It rains for three days, river rising so high that everything closes, from shops to canneries to packing sheds, and everybody goes home. The *Sacramento Bee* proclaims in screaming letters: Record Rains Threaten Levees! but no one sends engineers. Decades of work, swing by swing and shovel and scoop, have broken up this wet land and wound it through with hundreds of miles of dirt paths. The same minute-by-minute concern will save it. Men hustle from their homes every hour to check the levees for boils and breaks—arise even in the night with lantern light swinging before them, raincoats over their pajamas, and check the unsteady dirt already weakened by burrowing animals. If the levees go, Locke, built on reclaimed land that still thirsts for the water that used to course across it, will be washed away.

ON THE FOURTH day, the levees break.

42

SHELTER IS PROMISED, a mile down the road, in Walnut Grove. A man yells from the back of a truck, playing a siren salvaged off an old cop car, rousing people from their homes. The levee is crumbling. The town will flood. He is a doomsayer with the premonition of an hour and the weatherman on his side. Water seeps between the stacked sandbags. With any shoes they can find and anything they can carry, people begin to walk out of Locke.

Poppy hears the warning wail up and down the street and the water slither through cracks. She is a doomsayer of another sort, a soothsayer who finds the source of this trouble in three women. Superstition says that those who die by drowning will seek the living to take their place. Poppy prefers this version to weather reports of an unusual summer storm. She will stay. She chooses known to unknown, mud-choked town to exposed road. Drive out the women and the levees will heal themselves. She carries a metal barrel up the stairs. She'll burn dead money in the attic. High enough for safety and saved by smoke from spirits.

On the narrow attic stairs, she stumbles. The barrel clangs to the floor. Ashes spill in dunes across it. The rustling in the attic above stops. She steps back down the stairs and tries to sweep the ashes with her hands. It is soft fur in her hands, coats her palms in gray.

She tries again. Scrambling up the stairs, barrel hugged to the chest. The water will never find her. At the base of the stairs, the smudge of her efforts lies like a large, dark continent.

RICHARD PLEADS WITH Ming Wai that they stay.

We live on the second floor, he says. We'll be fine. He is loath to rise from bed, to dress, and to walk, hunched and weak, all the way to Walnut Grove. But Ming Wai pleads and crouches beside the bed and clasps his hand and insists, We must go, we must go.

Richard closes his eyes again. He hears the slide of the suitcase as Ming Wai pulls it out from under his bed. She checks the clasps. He lifts his head, leans forward, looks out the window. Already bits of people's lives float in the street—papers, a child's doll, unmatched shoes. Main Street has become a muddy trough that spreads itself against the sandbags lining the buildings. Rats scurry to the tops of the sandbags. The feeling of hurry descends. His feet slap the floor, and he goes to the kitchen first.

There is the swirling-chest panic of what to take and what to leave behind. Richard reaches for a box of crackers. Inside, a fat roll of bills and some silver coins. He runs back to the bedroom, distracted for a moment by the stiffness in his knees and wrists.

This too, he says, and hands the box to Ming Wai to put in

the suitcase. He flings open the wardrobe door and glances over his meticulous suits, his shiny shoes. These can be replaced. Only the suitcase. Only the suitcase cannot be replaced. He pulls a tin-cloth coat over his sleep clothes.

When they throw open the front door, they see that the water has already risen above the bottom steps. Ming Wai gasps. She holds the suitcase above her head, like a washer-girl with a basket. Richard leans against the rail. The water hits calf-deep. They slog through.

On Main Street, people lug china, paper, clothes, photos, silverware, packed into rice sacks, flour sacks, potato burlap, asparagus crates. Men lift children onto their backs. Women heft children onto their hips, nudged alongside a bag of precious things. Water runs from the roofs. Rust washes from metal patches. Water spirals down from the higher road into town. The paint looks brighter; the buildings are waking in the rain.

CHLOE RUNS DOWN the stairs and into the red room. She lifts the window and leans out. Rain comes in all around her, turning the pink curtains red, puddling on the floor. She gazes out over the street. People dressed for a day at the beach, at the fair. Clothes to sweat in, to play in. Some in mismatched pieces, put on in the dark, with an eye to the minute after. Choreography only in the exits. They exit alleys, doorways, porches. People come out, arms loaded. A family of cats yowls on the seat of a half-submerged chair.

Chloe shuts the window and nearly slips on the water around her feet. She catches herself and hurries out of the room. The door across the hall is shut. Chloe grabs the knob, puts her ear to the door before she knocks. There are people inside, oblivious to the rain. Chloe scoffs at her own shock. Of course sex still happens in the rain. She knocks lightly, just in case, then runs back upstairs.

In the corner, Madam See screams firework sounds against the rain and claps stained hands. She looks crazed, and Chloe feels shame for her.

Madam See! Let's go! Let's leave!

Madam See squints back at Chloe.

Let's go! We're packing! Chloe says.

Madam See shakes her head. She turns back to her fire and song.

Chloe's been planning to leave anyway—her bag has been packed for a week. She grabs her jacket, and pauses as she watches the other women. Lisel rolls up a poster pulled off the wall, Beatrice tosses trinkets into her pillowcase.

Are you mad? she asks. Beatrice pauses. The light through the window behind her halos her brown hair red. You don't need that. You should just go. We should just go. Chloe shakes her bag a little to settle the insides.

Beatrice rolls her eyes and puts a ceramic ballerina in her bag. She clears out other things from the tiny table next to her bed.

You don't have time, Chloe says. The water's already through the door.

Beatrice slows her hand. Lisel shakes out her bedding and spins it into a heap. Neither of them speaks to her. Beatrice looks Chloe up and down, then glances at Chloe's fat, full bag.

The distance between them now. When Chloe first came, she'd sometimes crawl into Beatrice's bed, fit herself against her body. Chloe knows she looks like someone who thinks herself too good. An apology catches in her throat. She drops the bag on her bed, grabs her jacket, and runs out of the room.

THEY WALK ALONGSIDE a river that frolics with spitting rage. Small boats tied up at the opposite bank knock together and pull against their tethers. Cars rumble past with people clinging to the sides, to the back. One boy, his feet safe from puddles as he rocks along on the edge of a truck bed, waves and smiles. Drought then flood, flood then drought; this is the cycle. In the ten years Richard has been in California, the fear of drought haunted many of those years, when the snowmelt wasn't enough and the summers burned off the reservoir waters. Ming Wai touches his arm. She smiles up at him. She blinks away raindrops.

What are you thinking of?

Richard shakes his head. He turns his face into the rain. Eight in the morning, but the sky looks like early evening and the birds are songless. Even from the first night, their wedding night, she held the look of someone too fragile to touch, someone he wanted to hurt. She gave herself up so easily, didn't even mew in protest when he shoved his fingers up between her legs. The rain lulls Richard. He is amused by the thought of Ming Wai's patient, scared breath.

A mile seems like ten in the drumbeat of the rain. An implied mutter rises up from the parade of small-town refugees, but when Richard looks behind them, he sees ranks of downcast eyes, set mouths, trudging feet. The crowd is chest-to-back in the traffic of evacuation. He hopes water will not leak through the seam of his suitcase. He coughs into his sleeve. With his thumb and finger, he rubs away dead skin from the corners of his mouth. He licks the rain from his lips, suddenly thirsty.

Hold my hand, Ming Wai says. Her voice is sweet. He sees a flash of blue beneath her coat. She's wearing her silk dress, bleeding electric blue into the gray day.

Aren't you cold?

A sudden anger wells up. She's flaunting her pleasure in the face of the group's misery. A refugee's trudge through the cold is a field trip to her—what lies over that path of water? What lies beyond this dip of land and town? She totters along, looking this way and that, smiling.

Hold my hand, she repeats. He can only comply. He takes her tiny bird wing into his hand and feels her hand like a burning ember in his palm.

The mismatched pace of an anxious family and Richard's ill shuffle opens up a space in the crowd. With the humming sound of whipped batter, the dirt turns to mud that turns to water. Before Richard can rear back, the road begins its slide into the river. Air eats its way through land. Half the road is suddenly missing. With his cough and dry throat and dizzy head, Richard thinks a second too late. He pinwheels his arms, feeling ridiculous even as he stumbles over the gap and into the water. He drops Ming Wai's hand, also too late. With a wail, Ming Wai comes tumbling after.

A splash of icy water. His coat fills and weighs him down. He fights his way out. His hands catch in the sleeves. He shakes until the coat blossoms away and sinks. He has lost his direction, can't find the shore, either by fumble or sight. My wife. The thought strikes him. Years pass as he treads his way through the spitting water and looks for Ming Wai. There she is, her hair spread around her like moss. She lures him over with her smile. My wife, my wife. She can't swim, he remembers. He swims toward her, pushing through the wet papers that have burst from his suitcase, his body growing heavier with every stroke.

CORLISSA WALKS ALONGSIDE her daughter. In San Francisco, there'd been sirens, a tentative crawl down the fire escape as the smoke threatened too close, but not this. Not so much water that mud washed into the house and the rugs soaked. The water there is contained, herded by the beach. She tells Sofia, Don't walk so close to the edge. Come in a little, So. Sofia clutches her arm. Howar glances over at her and gives a tired smile. His smile, the smile shared between two parents in a moment's claim on intimacy, barely clears his daughter's head. Their family—the triangulation of adult, adult, and child—is being refigured between three adults with the eye to judge. Sofia senses her exclusion and quickly looks up at her mother with the hint of a scowl pushing at her eyes.

Corlissa says quickly, It's just rain. The comment belongs in no conversation, a line exposed as a feint.

Sofia rolls her eyes. She turns her head and tiptoes for glimpses through the crowd as she shuffles forward with her mother. Who's she looking for? Corlissa turns too. She turns in time to catch the collective gasp, the single shout, the accompanying wail, the subsequent panicked push. The caravan of travelers stops for the sideshow.

Someone has fallen. Howar rushes into the crowd before Corlissa can call Stop! Sofia faces the trouble, but her eyes draw away to other parts, still searching. The two boat-women press themselves to Corlissa. So Wai covers her mouth. Corlissa takes it for horror.

She holds out her hand. Don't worry.

The two women draw even closer. So quick that it could be imagination, the women push her. Corlissa stumbles. Her shudder throws off Sofia's hand.

She twists her ankle on the edge of the crumbling levee and slips down the side. She presses herself to the dirt. Her body weight will slow her. All those circled thoughts of falling into the levee now realized: when driving, the dizzy focus of the wheel on the river's edge, the daring to speed off. Now on her own feet she's made it true. Confronted with the clear gray day of her nightmare, she can only give in to the fall, wait for the water. Commotion and sliding mud above her—rescuers or other unlucky ones—then the splash. The water sucks her under. She paddles her way up through current and over a froth of water. Back beneath again. She's been fighting blind. She opens her eyes. Water-blue women are below with her, bubbles lighting on their skin. She stops her thrashing. It might be lovely to stay.

Her first thought in the stream that comes in the body-lit dark beneath the surface is looking up at her mother's face as she lay in a tub of soapy water, no desires beyond food and drink and sleep. She saw the mildewed ceiling above her mother's head, the dun light, and the magic of her own foot rising pudgy from the water, a delightful plaything. Her mother's hand on her stomach, warm and big, and Corlissa uttered, Ma, which made her mother laugh.

Corlissa shakes her head. The water squeezes the air from her lungs. Sai Fung floats before her. She smiles at Corlissa and reaches for her. Corlissa knows that the extended hand, algae-soft and waterlogged, offers safety. Sai Fung's hair swirls softly, tangled with twigs, leaves, river trash.

Two hands. Holding hands. Corlissa fights whatever Sai Fung is trying to tell her. She thinks, instead, of her first day at school, locked in a dark coat closet during recess by another girl. Dirty-knickers, dirty-knickers, the girl taunted. Corlissa could feel the unbodied coats within, and pleaded through the door with her hand seeking out the held-tight knob. She screamed. The teacher opened the door and the whole class stared at her tear-stained face.

So Wai swims toward her and flashes a smile that looks green in the depths. Corlissa feels as if she's being courted— Sai Fung on one side, So Wai on the other. The edges of her vision gray toward black. She tries to kick toward the surface, but So Wai holds her back. Corlissa swears that she hears So Wai's voice: He said he would be back.

He said he would be back, but neither of them could account for the capriciousness of laws. In the mornings, she combed her mother-in-law's hair, brought her tea and a soft-boiled egg in rice soup. She swept the floor, then went out to the post office to see if any letters had arrived. Nothing had come since November. It was now January. She decided she must look for him and her mother-in-law agreed. She would leave in April; her twenty-four-carat gold bracelets would gain her passage and forged papers.

The two women embrace her. Their hold feels like her daughter's arms around her, needing her as if Sofia is five or ten again, when a mother's love is more treasure than curse. They need her. Corlissa relaxes into their grip and like a stream of music, their stories enter her thoughts.

They entered the boat in the middle of a moonless night. Each of them hammered into crates like pieces of chinoiserie. Through the slats of the crates, through the sweet smell of yellow straw, there was the musk of the cows and the mildew of the damp room.

Eventually, they pushed against the nails, lifted the lids, and peeked out.

They heard the strike and sizzle of a match and one of them lit a candle to a litter of scared faces—men and women—and even a solemn-eyed child on whose flesh the importance of silence had been beaten.

Most days, they sat still in their crates and left only to shit with the cows.

When the days one man had ticked off with the soot of a match-head equaled the number of days they knew it would take to reach their destination, they heard a shudder. They reached their hands through their crates and felt damp walls. As the cows began lowing and the chickens fluttered, the water seeped through the straw they sat on. The water crept up their ankles. Fearful of being caught, they remained silent until the water circled their chests. Who knows if the people stomping about in panic above heard them through the boards and the rush of water?

There was only cold and darkness.

To stay here, surrounded by mermaids and memories. She knows why they chose her. They risked life for hearsay. She tries to hold on to her desire for water, her yearning for gas, her hunger for branches. Sai Fung and So Wai press against Corlissa, whispering in her ears like reeds. More memories flutter by and then, finally, there is this: saved at the church

where she met Howar. An old man dunking her into a bathtub set up in the central room of the building. Beneath the
water, silence. Drawn up, dripping. People clapping. Approval
shining in Howar's eyes. The man's gravel-rough words as he
pulled her out. That which is born of the flesh is flesh. You
must be born again. You're saved.

Corlissa kicks and fights, feels their hands slipping over her
ankles.

We need you,

and then there is a plunge,

and the press of another body against her.

MING WAI IS just within reach. Richard lunges toward
her with a mmmph! of his weak body. His hands slip under
her shoulders. Her weight drags him down. They fall under
the murky water. He kicks harder. Her hands grab his waist.
They dance in the water for the life of one or both. He doesn't
know if she is fighting with or against. Her body is dead weight
under his hands. Her fingers press harder into his waist. The
banks disappear, the levee gone. Only river and his wife. Some
primeval instinct keeps him holding on. My wife. He takes a
breath and a second later they are both swept beneath again.
He hungers for air, but he does not let go of her. Beneath the
surface the clear water is a surprise.

There are so many of them down here—bodies snagged
on underwater roots, clothes caught on branches or between

rocks like webs. Ming Wai whispers in his ear: Fong Man Gum—breaking through the heartbeat quiet of water-rush and he wants to sleep to the sound of her voice.

He opens his mouth to respond and water fills it. With a start, he realizes the incongruity of her voice with the underwater world. A water ghost. He has been living with a water ghost. The words that can't even be spoken, only called, in a whisper, with euphemisms. His wife. She's found her place in a superstition. A servant to the water god, exchanging her life for that of another. His.

He wants to weep when he pushes away her hands. She holds on to his arm. The fingers settle, one by one. The lightness of her land-touch is gone.

He cannot leave. He becomes her. She had barely known him before he left. She shivered beneath him on the last night, her last chance to secure her position in the household with a baby boy. But there was no baby, and living in the house of his younger brother, she lost all status. In the stories floating through the household, around the tables, and through the ears and the mouths of the servants, he was not the noble son on Gold Mountain. He was the ne'er-do-well who had left his wife on their wedding bed.

She mended clothing and cleaned the toilets while the servants watched. She went to parties where women wore the latest European fashions and sucked on cigarettes in long holders, and when they danced, she sat, afraid for her reputation. And then one whispered to her a way to get to America. Ming Wai slipped off her gold bracelet and gave it to the woman with the bright red lipstick and permed hair. The woman kept her eyes on Ming Wai as she bit into the bracelet—red curving around gold—and Ming Wai's heart began to shake.

Richard thinks of her unsympathetic voice at their kitchen table: I lost face—how do you remedy that?

Ming Wai pulls his hand to her eyes. Richard relents.

He relents because of the smell of urine coming acid through yellow straw, the oven heat and ice cold that bore down for a month without relief. He relents because of the nights he spent not thinking of home, the days he spent making plans to never return. He relents when she pulls his arm around her neck, when his heart thumps against her hollow chest and her hair tangles in front of his eyes. She presses her mouth to his and he is kissing his wife. He holds the moment until he feels himself go limp in bursts of joy and pleasure that pop and pop. The words I love you do not come to him; instead, he thinks, like the rush of a deep-sea current: I'd give my breath to you.

Her hand closes into a fist at the back of his head, strands of his hair bristling out between her fingers. The tenderness of his scalp pulses and fades. His toes and legs empty out. She holds him tighter. His stomach calms. He forgets air. His head goes light. He fades until she is so full she must push him away and let him shimmer to the bottom of the river. She lunges up, crowns through the surface, and gulps air.

43

CORLISSA SWEEPS SALT and dried mud from the church floor in preparation for the funeral. She has swept it off the chairs where So Wai and Sai Fung slept and gathered it from the corners of the room into a small pile in the center.

Just as she had begun to struggle upward, she'd felt the push of a diving body. Arms wrapped around her. A man dragged her to the surface. People were waiting with ropes to pull them out of the water, but the rescue was too slow for the other two women. She knows now she has been death-touched that she should take a new joy in the day, but all she can think of is the missing bodies of the two women, and Richard's body on ice in the living room. His mouth has been sewn shut, the river debris combed from his hair. People have been in and out all day, talking of death. There's death on the cross, death in the body salt, death in the living room. Corlissa wishes she could let the talk fall around her, ignore the dust settling on the furniture, and take pleasure in fiddling with her daughter's hair, or watching her sleep. That is how miracles would affect storybook mothers.

But this is what Corlissa thinks of instead: being beneath the water. Edging her shoulder under a limp body, nudging a woman toward the surface as her own body sinks. She pauses in her sweeping to hold her breath and imagine the pain of airless lungs. She looks around quickly to see if anybody has seen her. She has never noticed before how the church windows, with their trapped bubbles, make the light look blue. She drags her broom over and looks out on a blue world. Red roosters tinted purple; leaves turned the color of sea foam.

She leans against her broom and breathes again. She looks toward the pulpit. It needs flowers. The Christ on the cross behind the pulpit hangs with strained tendons. She'll have to buy flowers.

LATER THAT AFTERNOON, she sits near the front of the church, dressed in funeral black. When Howar speaks in a calm monotone about the brevity of life but the eternity of heaven, she looks at Richard's widow and his friends. Ming Wai keeps her eyes on Howar. Corlissa fastens on the slow steady pulse in Ming Wai's neck. There seems to be no shaking, no inside break. Farther down, Manny Chow swipes the back of his hand to his eyes, pinches his nose with the other. The other men of the Lucky Fortune are the same: nostrils flared, tears falling, a rupture in their usual liquored, smoke-tainted bravado.

Sofia sits beside Corlissa, glassy-eyed, as if viewing an alternate fate. Someday, Sofia will leave home and it will be only

Corlissa and Howar again. They will pass each other in the same way—Howar off to do this or that, Corlissa off to straighten a cushion or polish the cabinet knobs again—but there will be no common subject. Corlissa will not say, Sofia did this today and Howar will not smile, or reach out to touch Corlissa's wrist when she tells her story. A photograph of Richard is propped against a vase of flowers. He rarely smiled in life; he doesn't smile in the picture. His hair is slicked flat, shiny. His eyebrows arch in a cocky way, and his skin is as smooth as the photograph paper. What was the meaning of his life? Corlissa glances again at Ming Wai, at Richard's friends. Prostitutes line the wall, alongside those who lost money from Richard and those who won. The value of his life defined by his mourners? A church full of passive town members? Corlissa wonders about the little redemptions in his life, because she knows only of the larger shape: he lived, he sinned, he died. That is as much meaning as Corlissa can give and she prays for his soul.

THE ECHO OF his voice flutters up from the floorboards. Poppy looks up from the mud-swollen ledger where she marks down numbers next to a yellow light and listens to Richard's voice speaking unclear words until the memory hides itself again in another part of the brothel. All her burned spirit money, the chants she cried as the river rose, made no difference. She was in the attic calling out superstition while just two hundred yards away he was drowning. She saw nothing.

She didn't catch any panic or pleasure drifting over the crumbled levee. This grief is worse than regret or ghosts.

In the quiet, she hears the rustle of Chloe's leaving. It is Chloe's body that lassos up the sounds and the phantom scents. When Chloe leaves, she will carry Richard away with her. Poppy tries to think her way upstairs, into Chloe's mind. She can get only as far as the stairs, where straggler ghosts—the last to return to hell—linger, smoke, and gossip. She tries again to hear Richard's whisper. She begins to cry—a relief, because the house goes quiet and she is left with only her five senses, a stomach cramped by sadness, and a thudding in her head.

She shuts the book and takes up her scissors. When she flips back the magazine cover, pages with missing centers untwist, and already-cut pieces fall to the floor. She picks up the small, trimmed illustrations of children, a bicycle, a car, a house, a mowing machine. She arranges them on her desk. She flips through, still sniffling, looking for other luxuries of an imagined life. She works on appliances today. She glances at two pictures, one of Richard and one of herself, leaning side by side against the wall.

She has built a model house and placed it on a paper sheet of green lawn. Inside, she has attached these clipped pictures with a brush of glue. A four-poster bed for the bedroom, a toilet with a pretty brass chain to accompany the claw-foot bathtub. With paint, she's colored red trim around the windows. After she is done, she will unclasp the backs of the frames, take out the wood and glass, and carefully cut out her own face and

Richard's. Then she will burn all of it. Together, they will live as spirits in their finely appointed spirit home. Footsteps make her put down her scissors and turn off the light. She touch-walks her way from office to kitchen, brushing over warm brick stove, crumb-pebbled tabletop, smooth-wood doorway, fresh watermark. The black boots descending from the shadows of the stairs make her catch her breath and dab her eye. She bites her lip in anticipation of one last look. She's sure Richard's spirit must be wandering, dying as he had under such unfortunate circumstances. For a moment, she puts aside her resentment of Ming Wai, who crawled out of the river as dull and flawed as the rest of them in a living body.

It is only Chloe. Chloe pauses after each step to listen for any rustling throughout the house. She tucks some hair behind her ear and takes another step.

This is what the dreams of coyotes meant. Chloe is racing away; she is kicking up spirals of dust behind her. For now, Poppy's life exists in clipped paper, and she doesn't mind if Chloe leaves. But she wants to touch her first, to see if any last remnants of Richard will pulse into her vision. She misses him. As Chloe passes the doorway, Poppy reaches out her fingers and their tips crackle across Chloe's wrist. The colors are so bright that the sight of a new baby-life turning with a tiny red beat inside of Chloe flashes for only a moment before the vision shatters to black.

Chloe jumps and lets out a tiny whimper. Chloe whispers, You scared me, Madam See!

Poppy is still blinded—like the green blindness of coming indoors on a sunny day. She turns toward Chloe's voice. Leaving?

She hears only Chloe breathe for a few moments, then: Yes, I'm leaving.

That's fine, Poppy says. Better that you leave now.

Chloe thanks her. I'll write.

Without touching her, Poppy knows this will not happen.

Chloe sighs. Good-bye. Poppy listens to her walk away. Every so often, the world reshapes itself in a startling way. In a matter of days, she has lost Richard and Chloe. One she cared for very much, the other not at all. It was balance, the world trying for some logic in its transformation. The front door opens and shuts. Chloe is gone now. It may be months before Poppy finds her place among the new absences and creates a day that makes sense. In the meantime, she clings to the doorway and waits for her vision to return.

CHLOE KNOWS BETTER than to turn around for a last glance. She knows how the lure of nostalgia can hold one back like sheet-draped sofas and dust-streaked floors. But she hears a voice in the kitchen.

Don't worry, girl, it's coming. I see the head.

Madam See had crouched before her, lovely and glamorous despite her bloody hands. Chloe feels all her muscles tighten.

Then Richard's hand on her back, and it's been so long since anyone has touched her that she wants to cry. You can squeeze my hand, he says. She takes his hand and leans into him.

He whispers in her ear, You're doing good. You're very brave. Very good. Very, very good. Such coaxing, and then such pain as the baby's head finally comes through. She screams, Pull it out! but she wants to see it so badly—something she has made, the very first thing she has for herself. There is rushing all around her: hot water, a knife, twine, Madam See yelling in Chinese. Chloe looks up at the kitchen window, lances of light dancing on it, blurred figures walking past.

Chloe knows what came next. She opens the door and quickly walks through.

She can't believe Richard is gone, even though she saw his body in the church, hands pale and limp by his sides. But she doesn't care, she tells herself. She doesn't care about dead babies, or dead men, or girls who tease with wine on their breath. She spits on the stoop of Madam See's.

Under the levee-side porch, tangled up in weeds, is a bicycle she has salvaged from the trash heap behind town. The frame is slightly bent, but it rides okay, and the little bell on the handlebar even dings. She props up the bike and ties her bag on top of the torn basket with twine. She has left some things behind in order to have a bundle small enough to carry this way. The bag is askew, but it holds. She pulls two knots, nudges the bag, then rolls the bike carefully out into the alley.

The deaths have quieted the town. No sounds seep through the closed doors of the Ho Yoi Ling Sing or Lucky Fortune.

Lights burn in seemingly empty rooms. The bats are quiet tonight.

She closes herself to the light on the top floor of the building where Richard's widow lives, to the blue windows of the church, and to the soughing wind in the crab apple trees in Sofia's yard. Under Sofia's window, she gathers a few fallen crab apples. She rolls them in one palm. She tosses one against the window.

The light goes on. Sofia appears in the window, hair tied back for sleep, eyes squinting.

Can you come down? Chloe says.

Sofia nods. Sofia will come down, blanket around her shoulders, and Chloe will lure her to the oak with a bottle of rice wine and smokes. When Sofia says, Show me how the boys kiss, this time Chloe will show her. Her bruises have all faded. Chloe will unbutton her shirt, slide it over each shoulder, and everything will be rewritten.

But the questions scare themselves away from Chloe's mouth. No Why? or Where? or Will you come with? She knows twice over that leaving is better without good-byes. The crab apples fall from her hand in three tiny thuds.

Chloe pushes the bike back across the lawn, between the houses, under the sycamores on Main Street, on the packed-dirt road with delicate steps over the still-lingering sludge puddles. She struggles up the hill past the mechanic's, where the oil stains shine like rainbows. On the river road, she steps on the pedal, pushes off, and swings her leg over.

The bike wobbles with its load, then steadies.

. . .

WHEN MING WAI leans toward the mirror, a smear of condensation clings to the glass. She wipes it with her sleeve and tries again. She begins and ends her days in awe of her own breathing.

On the first nights after they pulled Richard's body from the bottom of the river, she gathered his carefully hung clothes onto the bed and slept in the nest made of them. She breathed him in—her nose pressed to linen and cotton and wool and silk—until he was really gone, interred in the ground, no lingering odor left in the house. She wiped his fingerprints from the silverware and chopsticks and glassware. She sucked the bristles of his toothbrush until all she tasted was baking soda and her own spit. She burned paper money and paper houses and paper cars and paper women so that his afterlife would be too decadent to leave. And, once, she cried.

People come to mourn with her. She has lost two friends and a husband. She is too young, they cry, and she nestles herself easily into the role of virtuous widow. The Lucky Fortune gave her money, the stores provided groceries, and somebody else paid for a coffin.

Now she measures out her days with ritual. When she wakes, she yawns so deeply that there is pain in her lungs. If she is hot beneath the blankets, she opens the window and a breeze makes her cool. She watches her skin go from smooth to goose pimpled. She eats until her belly rounds out. She runs Richard's old toothbrush over her teeth and her gums and spits blood and foam into the sink. She urinates and shits and wonders at what her body uses and creates. Her hair and nails grow and her wounds scab over.

The walk to Richard's grave is slow on her broken feet and in the heat of an Indian summer. It takes her along the river that now flows smooth and quiet. The turned dirt is still fresh, but small shoots of grass have begun to grow. She thanks him for her tears and saliva and belches. She leaves fruit or meat offerings even though she knows her mouth is better suited for food than his.

She has even started bleeding again. She watches red drops bloom in the toilet water and thinks that maybe someday another life will come out of her own.

ACKNOWLEDGMENTS

The citizens of Locke warmly welcomed me to their town in the summer of 2000. For their stories, a special thank-you to Ping Lee and his family, Connie King, Everett Leong, Dustin Marr, Lillian Chan, Clarence Chu, and Ronnie. Thank you to John and the Sotos for food, drinks, and conversation. "The King" has kept me connected to the town ever since.

This has been a seven-year journey. My parents, Michael and Ellen, and my family (Tina, Annie, and Emily) were always supportive. Thanks to Lily Wang, Yosefa Raz, Augustus Rose, Bridget Hoida, and especially Kyhl Lyndgaard and Renee Osborne. Spring Warren was an inspiring writing partner. Dan Leroy was my Delta plant resource and guide. Jenny, Jeffrey, and Heather from 626B have been with me since the very beginning. Jia Ching Chen provided love, food, and shelter as I searched for a home for the book.

The U.C. Davis Consortium for Women and Research and the Poon Foundation generously funded the research for this book. Early on, Anne Cheng talked me through the book's racial/political issues. Clarence Major, Pam Houston, and Wendy Ho provided invaluable intellectual support and feedback. Gary Snyder and the dearly missed Carole Koda kept me well stocked in books on Chinese myths and poetry. My fellow students of the U.C. Davis M.A. class of 2001 helped see me through the original first chapters of the book, and John Lescroart and Lisa Sawyer's generous endowment of U.C. Davis's Maurice Prize in fiction came at exactly the right moment for a struggling writer.

Finally, I'd like to express my deep gratitude to the two homes *Locke 1928* has had. First, to Thomas Farber, Kit Duane, and Andrea Young at the independent press El Leon Literary Arts, who gave the book its first home in 2007; and then, to my agent, Daniel Lazar at Writers House, who believed in and championed the novel, and to Jane Fleming at The Penguin Press, who has given the book a second life. I am forever grateful to you all.

I would like to credit the following:

The Young Jade story that the boat-women tell to Sofia is a retelling of a version found in *The Golden Casket: Chinese Novellas of Two Millennia*, translated by Christopher Levenson from Wolfgang Bauer's and Herbert Franke's German version of the Chinese (Penguin Books, 1967). The original "Young Jade" is credited to Liu Shih-yin. Other details of Chinese myths were found in *Chinese Mythology: An Introduction* (Johns Hopkins University Press, 1993) by Anne Birrell and *Sole Survivor* (Design Enterprises of San Francisco, 1985) by Ruthanne Lum McCunn. Information on Chinese ideas of death (and connections to sexuality and status) were found in *Death Ritual in Late Imperial and Modern China* (University of California Press, 1988), edited by James L. Watson and Evelyn S. Rawski.

Details of life in the Delta were found in *Delta Reunion 1999: End of the Century Memory Book*, a collection of memories and pictures put together for the 1999 reunion. Carole Koda's *Homegrown* (Companion Press, 1996, limited edition) also provided data about growing up in a Valley farming community. Ron and Peggy Miller's *Delta Country* (La Siesta Press, 1971) was a source for information about the sloughs and waterways, as well as plant and animal life.

For information about the Chinese in America and the history of exclusion laws, I consulted *The Chinese at Home and Abroad. Together with the Report of the Special Committee of the Board of Supervisors of San Francisco, on the Condition of the Chinese Quarter of that City* (A. L. Bancroft, 1885) by Willard B. Farwell; Shirley Fong-Torres' *San Francisco Chinatown: A Walking Tour* (China Books and Periodicals, 1991); *Pigtails and Gold Dust* (Caxton Printers, 1947) by Alexander McLeod; *Lotus Among the Magnolias: The Mississippi Chinese* (University Press of Mississippi, 1982) by Robert Seto Quan with Julian B. Roebuck; and *Claiming America: Constructing Chinese American Identities During the Exclusion Era* (Temple University Press, 1998) by K. Scott Wong and Sucheng Chan.

For information on the role of women in the 1920s, I relied on *Unbound Voices: A Documentary History of Chinese Women in San Francisco* (University of California Press, 1999) by Judy Yung; *Fighting the Traffic in Young Girls* by Ernest A. Bell (various versions by different presses exist; I looked at a 1930 version); *Women and the American Experience*, Vol. 2, from 1860, 2nd edition (McGraw-Hill, 1994) by Nancy Woloch; and *If They Don't Bring Their Women Here: Chinese Female Immigration Before Exclusion* (University of Illinois Press, 1999) by George Anthony Peffer.

For further reading on Locke, see former U.C. Davis professor Peter C. Y. Leung's *One Day, One Dollar: Locke, California and the Chinese Farming Experience in the Sacramento River Delta* (The Liberal Arts Press, 1994); the exquisite photo essay by Jeff Gillenkirk and James Motlow, *Bitter Melon: Inside America's Last Rural Chinese Town* (Heyday Books, 1987); and fine publications from the Sacramento River